This novel was written in 2019. For more info... n the author and his journey to writing his first novel, please scan the QR code or visit his website. Enjoy the read!

JAMES-GUNN.CO.UK

To Valerie

Thank You For Always Listening

xx

Shall Joy wear what Grief has fashioned?

- Oscar Wilde

CHAPTER 1

Gerry was a cunt. He came over to London from Dublin when he was about 21, married the first woman who let him into her bed, had some kids, drank some Guinness, sat in the Gentlemen's clubs in Harlesden in the '60s and '70s and plotted with his fellow oppressed man how to end the 'No blacks, no dogs, no Irish' sentiment in England at the time. In fact, in the first ever social club he set up, he was the only white man, the rest were black. He was apparently looked at like some kind of Irish Eminem, without the Slim Shady bleach blonde hair and the poetry. Gerry was anything but slim; he was quite the hefty man who had as much respect for the English as he did for his BMI level. He was shady though and throughout the years, I've realised that despite his best efforts to paint himself as some kind of Irish Braveheart fighting against the powers that be, he would have bloody thrown his black pals under the proverbial bus if the English let him into their pubs to begin with.

He wasn't a racist; he hated black people as much as he hated his own mother. It wasn't a race thing; he just didn't like people. Full stop. Even his wife Cheryl, whom he loved, was one egg being cooked sunny-side-up away from being divorced and thrown into a guillotine. He had this switch where one second you were his best pal and the next you were being accused of being involved with the 'Japs' (as he put it) during Pearl Harbour. The amount of times I had to sit him down and explain to him that I wasn't even alive during the Second World War, let alone dropping bombs on Ben Affleck and Josh Harnett, was too many times to be acceptable.

Gerry didn't like me. I know what you're thinking: 'How on earth could someone not like such a handsome, loveable, hilarious chap, such as yours truly?'

Well he didn't. My gut feeling is Gerry was a bitter man who disliked the fact that his daughter was born and bred in England, fell in love with an English boy and would go on to have little English sprogs. Plus, the only thing Irish about Gerry's daughter, is that she loves Westlife. But who doesn't, am I right? He may have also hated me because when I was drunk one Christmas, I whispered in his ear during the Queen's Speech, "I know you're a paedophile."

He had already had three strokes by this time, and I wasn't fully sure if his reaction to this comment was a scowl or a slight grin. Let's, for the good of my own conscience, say it was a grin. We finally clicked; after years of trying, it was the paedophile joke that got him to love me. Or, he was just a paedophile. And if that was the case, he died a hero, just like Jimmy Saville. Saville, of course, died never being caught, a huge hero's ceremony with people throwing flowers at his coffin and lining the streets to praise him. Imagine being one of those people now? Knowing the truth. And that could be you guys today...

Gerry's dead. Cancer of the oesophagus. I'm practising my speech (adding stuff I want to say but won't when the time comes) in the mirror at his funeral, backstage at St Phillip Neri's Church in London. Phillip Neri was the Patron Saint of Mirth. Mirth means amusement (especially expressed in laughter). This fact, in about one minute's time, will be a great irony. I know about Neri because I stumbled upon his name on Wikipedia about 401 link clicks in, during one of those Sunday night sessions where you're bemoaning the fact you have to get up at 7am Monday but you've begun reading pointless shit at 11pm and you've started to enjoy it too much at 3am. I can't remember where I started but I found myself reading about Larry Flynt and then clicked onto 'Vulva' (of course I did, I'm a man and there's diagrams). I then, for some inexplicable reason, decided I needed to know about the history of the 'Tampon'. At no point in my 30+ years on the planet had I ever even considered educating myself on such a matter, but on this night, I needed to know. From Tampon, I clicked 'Cervical Mucus' (who wouldn't?) and from there, I kind of went back and forth from a lot of pages with information that will lead me in good stead for my current predicament. Not speech writing, but parenthood. I ended my education on the perils of the female anatomy and childbirth on 'Caesarean Section', because I accidentally clicked into 'Rome', and from Rome, I noticed 'Saint Philip Neri', a name I was familiar with due to walking past the church on most weekends visiting my girlfriend's parents. The reason I knew what mirth meant was because I googled it. If I don't understand a word or reference, I google it, and that's the best advice I'll give anyone ever. Google it if you don't get it because getting it is much better than pretending to get it.

As I press delete in my mind on all the Cervical Mucus I never want to see again, I try to find a pen in my pocket to make a slight tweak to my speech. Before I can make amendments, I see my girlfriend Rosemary, Gerry's daughter, waddling up from behind the curtain towards me. She's eight months pregnant and her face, as usual, is one of a woman who appears to be becoming a human teapot with every step. This time, however, she's actually steaming from the top of her head. I look at her and shrug, as if to say, "What can I have possibly done now? There's no bloody pillows in the church that need to be fluffed for you and your arthritic back."

She grabs the speech from my hand, throws it to the floor and says whilst scrunching her hot flushed little face up, "Your mic…is on."

The awkward tension in the air as I arrive at the wake (being held at Gerry's last social club he owned) is on par with the tension I felt when my own father died. Mainly because in the same moment his life support did the dead beeping flatline thing, I was fluffing up his pillow, and in that same moment, my mum and sister both walked into the room to witness a scene which looked like some back-alley Dignitas. To this day, they still make jokes that I finished him off, but I didn't. Promise.

Rosemary is mingling, which means I'm pretty much left alone to fend off the gazes of all the other guests whom I had moments earlier basically called paedophile sympathisers. I try to get her attention so she will come and stand with me so I don't look like Tom Hanks in *Castaway,* slowly wasting away by myself. He was lucky to have Wilson; I have nobody. Every time Rosemary and I make eye contact, she shakes her head in disappointment and thus confirming what I knew when I walked in the room; everybody hates me, and this is going to be a long night. Whilst standing at the bar waiting to get a drink, a little old lady approaches me with only a Zimmer frame preventing her from kissing the floor quite heavily.

"Young man," she says whilst taking one hand off the Zimmer and gesturing for me to come nearer to her.

I step closer to the old bird (grabbing her hand and putting it back on the Zimmer when I reach her). At this point, I'm expecting an earful off everyone and if I start with a little old lady who will say what she really means, it'll lessen the blows of others who may filter their thoughts down because we are at a funeral after all. She leans in; I can feel her prickly beard on my cheek.

"That speech was fucking beautiful," she whispers.

I lean back in shock and look at her with my brows squeezing down tightly against my eyelids due to the utter confusion of what she just said. She winks at me. I smirk.

"Thank you," I say reluctantly, whilst nodding my head and for some reason curtsying in front of her.

She laughs. This isn't as bad as I thought it was going to be. I have a fan!

"Congratulations," I hear another woman's voice from behind me say.

I turn around and a stern-looking woman in her late twenties/early thirties is staring me down with her piercing blue eyes, which is now making me think that things are going to be as bad as I thought they were going to be.

"For what?" I mutter, like a scared little boy who's just been caught raiding the biscuit tin.

"For being the deadest person at a funeral," she grins.

She's laughing at her own joke. I don't entirely get it, but I do a scared awkward laugh anyway. I feel a tap on my back and turn around to see the old lady looking at me.

"That's my daughter, Ava."

I look back towards Ava. "Hi Ava, I'm John." I go to shake her hand, "My mates call me Johnny though and my mum calls me John, so ..."

She shakes my hand back, whilst butting in before I can finish, "I'll have to decide whether I'm your mum or your mate?"

"Yeah something like that I guess."

"Well my mum felt sorry for you and now I do too, so we're seeing if you want to come and join us at the delinquents' table over there?"

Ava points at an empty wooden small table in the corner which hasn't been decorated and has two plates of food on it looking like something out of *Oliver Twist*.

"Mum and I didn't really know Gerry that well but we just like going to funerals," Ava said.

Lord, I'm speaking to the female version of the Will Ferrell character in *Wedding Crashers*, and why am I comparing everything to movie references? I need a drink, so I just say yes to joining them.

Sitting at the delinquents' table is probably the best I could have hoped for to be honest. It turns out the old lady's name is Caroline and she actually did know Gerry. They dated in Ireland before Gerry came over here. Caroline followed but by the time she found him, he had already settled down with Rosemary's mother, Cheryl. Caroline eventually met somebody else and had her only child, Ava. Ava and Caroline are obviously sitting here because Cheryl is being a vindictive little cow, but I like Cheryl, so I think it's pretty funny. I'm sitting here because I now have no friends and my girlfriend hates me. But whilst there is alcohol, there is hope.

I've never really understood funerals anyway, so I don't think I'm missing much due to my banishment. I mean, they're all doom and gloom, aren't they? Especially religious ones. They just bang on about how the dead person is now in Heaven and how it is all part of 'God's plan'. It's just bullshit. A friend of mine had a daughter who died not long after being born and at the funeral, I had to listen to the priest yap on about how although the baby was only alive for a few days, it was 'God's plan' to take her away from her parents earlier for 'bigger things'. I nearly stood up and said, 'Fuck God's plan'. I'd rather have my friend's kid back then to have her involved in some mysterious plan that we don't know about. In what other situation would we just accept that it's a good thing that a kid is being taken by some strange man who we haven't ever seen because he needs her for his plan that he's not telling us the details for? It's bullshit. Yeah, it might be comforting words to help with the grief but quite frankly, I'd rather be told the truth; life isn't fair and it's fucking heartbreaking.

The other thing that bugs me about funerals is the fact that everyone wears black. Who invented that as a thing? It's just bleak. My favourite colour is black, and I still don't get it. You're sticking a corpse in the ground and covering it in mud; you don't have to make that situation even more grim by wearing black, playing haunting hymns and having a big old black car procession slowly holding up traffic in the street on the way to the graveyard. Not to mention that funerals cost an absolute fortune. Ripping off the bereaved in their time of need; how do these fuckers live with themselves? I've told Rosemary already, should I die, throw me in the bin and use the money to go on holiday instead. I'm honestly not worth the debt.

Although I'm aware that Rosemary wouldn't think twice about throwing me in the bin alive today, I still try to grab her attention from my seat as she talks to DJ Davey D. DJ Davey D is the resident DJ at the social club for any parties and also just broke up with his second wife after he found her in bed with his dad. His real name is David Donaldson and he's a 40-something-year-old bloke currently going through a mid-life crisis (of course he is, he just found his wife in bed with his dad). He thinks he's Tiesto and is planning to go to Ibiza this summer to 'get work' and 'do a season'. This is the first time he's been asked to do a funeral and his set is the only light relief in what has so far been a very joyless affair. I've already upset DJ Davey D by actually saying hello to him and saying, "This is a joyless affair, isn't it?"

Turns out 'affair' is a trigger word for him, and he had to go for a cry in the bloke's toilets to compose himself before he set up his computer to play the playlist he created on Windows Media Player. Rosemary is comforting him and making sure he's alright whilst I try to give her the thumbs up from a distance to make sure he's okay to get the music going. I'm bored and there's only so much talking I can do with Ava about French films.

Ava loves French films. I've learnt this because she's just spoken to me about her interests for the last two hours like I give a shit. She's too friendly and too nice for me to stop her though, so thus far, I've learnt that she loves *Amélie*, *The Intouchables*, *The Artist*, *Blue is the Warmest Colour*, *The Class*, *Amour* and some other ones that I blanked out during her passionate recallings of. I also know that she's a huge fan of the French actress Marion Cotillard. Apparently, her performance in the film *La Vie En Rose* is one of the finest performances ever by a female actress. I haven't seen it, and therefore, again, I do not care. She also loves more of her films: *Love Me If You Dare* and another one called *Rust and Bone* where Marion's legs get bitten off by a killer whale or something and it's romantic. Not sure what's romantic about getting your legs gnawed off but I'll take her word for it. I made a witty quip about how "Gerry's going to be 'Rust and Bone' soon", but Ava just turned to me and told me how it can take around 12 years for a body to decompose in a coffin. Ruined the joke, but I saw Caroline grinning away like The Cheshire Cat. I think the old lady with the Zimmer frame might be my soul mate!

I also learnt that Ava likes folded over crisps, and mint creams. I also like mint creams, but I have no preference on whether my crisps are folded over or not. That's just weird. And just when I thought I stopped learning about this random woman I've had to spend the last two hours with, DJ Davey D, who has now fully recovered and reunited with his decks after weeping in the bathroom, starts playing a track; and Ava is up on her feet dancing straight away.

"I love Dave Matthews Band!" she screams.

I purposely pick up a folded crisp from the paper plate and chew it quickly.

"Who?" I ask, because I genuinely haven't heard of Dave Matthews, his band, or this song.

"Ants Marching Johnny, Ants bloody Marching."

Ants Marching? What is she going on about? Before I can find out, she grabs my arm, and drags me unwillingly to the dance floor where we are now dancing to an upbeat song at a funeral, surrounded by people who now hate me even more. Ava is loving it though, and from a distance, Caroline gives me a thumbs up, whilst out the corner of my eye, I can see Rosemary shaking her head disapprovingly.

And this is where it all starts. This dance, this beautiful brunette idiot, dancing in front of me. The end of Gerry's story is the beginning of mine. Dave Matthews, mint creams, folded crisps and French films.

Merde!

CHAPTER 2

We bring our son home from the hospital today. Samuel Jerry Thomas. I wanted him to have my name as a middle name, but Rosemary wanted to have her dad's. I suggested having both and she suggested no, and then we somehow agreed on spelling 'Gerry' with a 'J' which was sold to me as combining both our names. I lost this argument now I think about it, but I'm not going to fight with a woman who's just been in labour for nearly two days. Heroic would be an understatement of a word to describe how well Rosemary did in the hospital. Despite the bruises and the hands that belong to me being quite clearly broken due to her squeezing and other 'accidental' jolts my way, there wasn't really any drama or complications. The kid just didn't want to come out; he was being lazy, and quite frankly, I don't blame him. Who would want to come into today's world? Not me. I'd hide in Rosemary too if I could. Fuck having to listen to any more talk about Brexit; I'm staying inside Rosemary's vagina and I'm not coming out! It's warm, oh so warm.

I snap out of my daydream as I lift the car seat from the car and walk towards our flat which is above a newsagent's/greengrocer in Camden, London. Mo, who I've known since I was about 21, owns the shop and comes to greet us.

"Welcome home, yaaaay!"

"Hi Mo." I give a thankful nod.

"Mohammed," Rosemary says sternly as she stands next to me wanting to get in as soon as possible.

"I tried to get a few of the boys from the bookies and the kebab house to come and give you a hero's welcome at your door, but you know, they couldn't be arsed," Mo shrugs.

"Right, how nice of them," I say, as I start my walk towards the door to our gaff.

"Wait, wait, wait!" Mohammed stops me and runs back to grab a banana from a crate.

He brings it over and starts rubbing it on Samuel's little newborn head. "Baby wants a banana, baby wants a banana," Mo sings over and over again.

"He doesn't want a banana," Rosemary pipes up in frustration to the song. I kind of like it; it's catchy.

"Maybe one day," Mohammed nods and places the banana next to Samuel in the car seat.

"Thanks Mo," I smile and nod again.

Rosemary and I turn our backs and open the door which leads to a flight of stairs which then leads to our front door. Rosemary walks up the stairs to open the door whilst I wait at the bottom, watching Mohammed walk back to his shop whilst whistling the tune to his 'Baby Wants a Banana' song.

I've lived in this house since I was eighteen. If the walls could talk, they would tell you some stories for sure. They'd tell you about the time I nearly died because I left a candle burning in a room which I had just decorated. I went through an extended period of purchasing different scented candles to make the flat smell like something better than beer, sperm and regret. My friends would call this 'my gay phase' but there's nothing gay about nice smells. The house nearly burnt down, which has left a lingering whiff of smoke and the living room wall, which took the brunt of the damage, is now covered with Rosemary's art. She fancies herself as a bit of a Banksy and to be fair she's quite good. It was once covered by another Banksy, Gordan and the rest of the 1966 England World Cup winning squad, but that poster has long since been relegated to a box under the bed.

The bachelor pad didn't last long. Rosemary moved in officially two years after we got together but right from the start, she made herself at home. It started off with little things like vegetables turning up in my fridge when I don't really care for them and then quickly escalated into hair in my bath plughole. Hair in the plughole is the game changer. Once the hair is in the plughole, she's moved in. I knew this and yet it wasn't until Gordan and the boys of 1966 got put under the bed, did it truly hit me.

Many things make a home: family, a pet, the calming feeling of knowing that under your roof you know where stuff is, and you know where stuff goes. That calming feeling goes away when your girlfriend moves in. Cutlery is now found where I used to keep the beer pong tools and coats now get hung up on a coat rack instead of just thrown down anywhere. Things changed when Rosemary moved in, that's all I'm saying. The only thing that didn't change was my bed. Beds make homes. I love my bed and luckily, she loved my bed too; she still does. In fact, it got called 'our bed' very early into the relationship. When I first moved into the flat, I was sleeping on the sofa. I never went to college or university. I left school at sixteen and went straight into work. Nothing special, nothing that I cared about, just something that got me some money at the end of each month. By eighteen, I had saved enough to get a few bits and a king size bed was one of them. I'm over six-foot tall and have been since I was about six years old, I think, so whilst I appreciate that some people don't have a bed to sleep on at all, in my world, sleeping in a single bed for most of my life was a nightmare. The king size bed cost me £200 and the mattress cost me about £400. Over ten years later and it's still going strong. Despite not being as svelte as I was in my younger years, the bed has handled my beer gut and Rosemary's baby tummy. It has also managed to hold up the weight of the world which has been on my shoulders many times. The bamboo pillows and the duvet which have gone from having a Stone Cold Steve Austin WWF cover to a pink and white flowery cover are my favourite things to see after a long day. I love that bloody bed, and when I've been up or down in life, it's been there to cuddle me.

Ah, if walls could talk, eh? When I first moved in, they kind of did. My older, by two years, sister Katie and her boyfriend Dan came over to help me decorate. We scraped off the 1960s' wallpaper and as we did, a small little written message saying 'Jim and Dee lived here' was revealed behind it, scribbled onto some other wallpaper, with a love heart drawn next to their names. I often wonder who they were and how their story continued after they left this home. It's crazy, isn't it, to think about how many other people in time have lived in the same place as you, or walked the same streets, sat at the same bus stop, fell in love, cried, died. So many people have had a great story that we'll never know about and that's a pity.

Rosemary takes Samuel out of the car seat and lays him on the bed. He is so tiny and as I walk into the room, dropping some bags on the floor, I can already tell that he's going to look like his mum. She's blonde and has blue eyes and he has a slight sprinkling of fair hair already with the brightest blue eyes I've ever seen. This doesn't annoy me; I want him to look like his mum. Nobody wants to have my nose. It has very wide unusual nostrils and Rosemary says that if I fell from a plane, I'd survive because my nose would act as a parachute. It's a rude thing to say but it's probably true. Rosemary just watches Samuel lay on the bed; he's looking up at her whilst trying to chew on his own hand. I watch them both and walk towards the bed and sit down behind Rosemary, resting my chin on her shoulder.

"Be careful," she whispers softly.

"I will."

Before I started dating Rosemary, there wasn't an influx of females vying for my attention. I was disinterested in trying to live up to an expectation portrayed in romantic fairy tales. Therefore, when your peers only have an experience in love from books, films and Adele songs, it's tough to impress them with a relationship based within reality. I'm not that fucking great. I'm not going to be Ryan Gosling-style picking you up with my abs out and giving you the best sex of your life. I'll give you bang average sex with the three moves I know. (Me on top, you on top and you bent over the couch). That was my eighteen-year-old self's thought process anyway. It was probably based around an anxiety of not being good enough and a nervousness that I wasn't experienced at whatever it was someone else needed to be given to them. I lost my virginity at sixteen; it lasted about 44 seconds at a house party with a girl whom was known for sleeping about at school. For 34 seconds of that sexual experience, I was on the phone to my mum because she rang me mid-thrusting and I decided for some creepy reason to answer it. She just wanted to know when I'd be home. Never. I was going to kill myself that night because I had basically just lost my virginity to my mum.

My first real girlfriend was Naomi when I was seventeen; she was in the year above me at school, but we only really started talking when I left. I'd describe her as a cross between Rihanna, because she was born in Barbados, and Aileen Wuornos, because after a few months of dating, I sensed a bit of a serial killer vibe from her. She came to London at around five years old so at eighteen she was pretty much speaking with a London accent, but as her parents were full-on Bajans, she still had a twang when saying a few words. She often used to call me and shout down the phone, "Wuh part you is?"

This basically meant she was getting paranoid about me being out without her and she wanted to know where I was. I was probably in a pub watching football or out doing something unsubstantial with my friends, but to Naomi it didn't really matter; she wanted to know, and she wanted to turn up. She was mad, but I was seventeen and having sex with an attractive girl so I took the madness for as long as I could. It was only after she turned up at my parents' house with five suitcases containing all her belongings after she got kicked out of her house for smoking that I realised it was time to have the chat with her about how we were probably on separate paths in life. For example, I wanted the path where I lived, and she was probably on a path to mass murder and prison. I didn't say this to her obviously as I didn't want to be her first victim (if she hadn't struck already obviously). The mass murder, as far as I and the police are aware, never materialised actually, as Naomi has since set up a fashion advice business and has around 500,000 followers on social media; she did alright for herself in the end. One thing that did stay with me though was something she said the last time I saw her. As I followed her down the stairs (carrying four of her five suitcases) after the breaking up conversation, I stumbled and fell right to the bottom. She didn't help; she just waited for me to slowly get up to my feet as she gathered her stuff up which had partly been covering my aching body on the floor. I dusted myself down, eventually looking up to see her open my front door, and before she stepped out, she looked back at me and said, "Trouble don't set up like rain."

She then walked out, and I didn't see her for nearly fifteen years until recently where an advert popped up online with her face on it selling a goats' milk face mask. Don't ask.

I never really understood what Naomi meant back then, but I do now. Mainly because I've lived a life since then and partly because I googled it. One thing is for sure, the girl was right. Even if she was grammatically wrong.

The rest of my dating history is pretty piss poor to be honest. It consists of a few meaningless one-night stands and a few girls who I thought I was in love with, but it turns out I was young, stupid and knew absolutely nothing about what love was. Unrequited love, which poets of yesteryear will describe to you as the most romantic kind of love, isn't really love at all in my opinion. It's more like infatuation. It's not really love if the other person doesn't love you back because why would anybody love somebody who doesn't love them? An indifference to me these days wouldn't spark up a flame in my heart that would make me love someone who has such meaningless feelings towards my being. Yet, when you're young and stupid and just pretty clueless, unrequited love makes you act like a fool. There was Sophie who put me in the friend zone; then, there was Laura who kind of liked me but also liked shagging everyone else and then eventually put me in the friend zone. With Laura, I tried to win her heart by sending her gifts and writing her letters, which now

21

makes me cringe uncontrollably because it must have given her self-confidence a right good boost, when quite frankly, she was really a bit of a dickhead. I'd have much rather (in hindsight) crushed her confidence so she didn't want to leave the house again, but instead I wrote her a letter every day for six months, and all this whilst she clearly strung me along for free cinema trips and free food. Love is blind and all that. And I'm not bitter.

Maybe, during that time, I was a victim of my own upbringing and environment. Nobody taught me how to win a girl's heart; I just somehow thought I had to and so tried what I thought had to be done. Why couldn't I just accept Sophie just wanted to be my friend and Laura didn't want to run away and marry me and love me forever and ever? I'll tell you why: movies.

Romance movies always have blokes getting turned down and then spending the rest of the movie trying to change the girl's mind. More often than not, it goes one of two ways:

> 1) The guy shows the girl that what life has been missing all along is some chubby middle-aged man with great comedy timing.

> 2) The guy, along his journey of trying to change her mind, changes his mind and realises he loves another female character who's more suited to him and the

original love is painted out not to be that great after all and in some way kind of bad.

Why can't the girl just say 'NO'? End of film. Why can't she just be independent enough or know herself enough to say she does not fancy this bloke, never will; and him, whoever he may be, takes 'no' for an answer and realises there's no underlining issue to her saying 'no'; she just doesn't want it! She's not insecure, she's not hiding past relationship scars that need to be healed before she can love again, nor does she have some kind of attitude problem when it comes to men. She doesn't want to be wooed, she doesn't want him to keep pestering her for a date and when she's riding a big Ferris wheel, she doesn't want him to climb on top of it and hang off until she says yes to a date, because that's blackmail and blackmail is a crime. Furthermore, when she says 'no' and you find someone else, it doesn't make the girl who turned you down less than the new chick. It doesn't make her the bad character; it just means that she said 'no' and she doesn't have to justify it. It's all a bit rapey in my opinion. Anyway, all those girls were cunts and eventually I found Rosemary.

*****

Rosemary's getting ready for bed and I'm holding Samuel whilst lying under the covers. Brushing her teeth, Rosemary looks back at me with every stroke to make sure I'm holding our son the right way. Part of me wants her to turn around to see me holding him by the head like one of those amusement park machines where the claw tries to grab a teddy then drops it just before you win. I don't do that though. I just run my big man fingers through his little baby fingers and ignore the fact that my girlfriend doesn't trust me not to drop him or snap his neck. If anything, I hold him a little bit more gently, so when she turns around, she knows that he's safe with his dad.

*****

I met Rosemary at a bar located across the road from Chalk Farm station on a New Year's Eve night out which can only be described as 'Lionel'. That's what the kids these days would say anyway. It's a kind of rhyming slang for 'messy' because of Lionel Messi the Argentine footballer. Basically, I was very drunk.

I think you'll agree that New Year's Eve is always overrated. I much prefer St Paddy's Day, my birthday and the ultimate night out, Christmas Eve. Christmas Eve is the one where all your pals from over the years come back from wherever they are in the world and you all end up in that same pub talking about the good times whilst creating more good times. It ruins Christmas Day of course, because your hangover is still going strong when the standard death in EastEnders is happening, but it's bloody worth it. New Year's gets the hyped treatment but it's always expensive and by midnight, you're not really fussed about what's going on because you're either too drunk, reached that level of drunk where you're in the toilet giving yourself a life pep talk in the mirror, looking for someone to pull, or not drunk enough to enjoy everyone else around you being jolly. I wasn't drunk enough on this night in question, but I was still looking for someone to pull.

I felt like I was being pretty smooth sitting down at a table on my own watching everyone else dance whilst still making sure Rosemary knew I was looking at her. She was on the dancefloor, wearing a light blue dress and was dancing with her mates singing 'Mr Brightside' by The Killers at the top of her lungs. She couldn't sing, but she looked bloody good trying.

In the end, my mates were calling me up to the dancefloor by shouting 'boring' at me repeatedly. I noticed that Rosemary overheard this and looked over in our direction inquisitively. I didn't want her to think I was boring so I got up and walked into a bundle of drunken hugs from my friends as they cheered my arrival. I danced and sung my way through 'Grease Lightnin'' by the cast of the movie *Grease*, 'Hey Baby' by DJ Otzi and a selection of Oasis anthems, before it was time to wander back to the bar for some much-needed sambuca.

At the bar, I ordered myself four sambuca shots, which if you've ever been out in London on New Year's Eve, you'll know it cost me around fifty quid. I downed the first one and gave my head a bit of a wobble as it didn't go down too well. From behind me, I heard a drunk voice getting nearer and nearer singing...

"No matter what I do, all I think about is you. Even when I'm with my boo, you know I'm crazy over you."

I looked around and it was Rosemary stumbling towards me doing spins and singing 'Dilemma' by Nelly featuring Kelly Rowland. The song had just started on the dance floor, but she decided to come over and annoy me instead.

"I saw you looking at me," she said as she sat on a stool at the bar.

"I don't think I was," I muttered back still feeling the effects from the sambuca.

"You love me," Rosemary said in her drunken state which looked like she had lost control of the muscles in her face.

"I don't even know you."

"Yes, you do. I'm Rosemary," she grabbed one of my sambucas and necked it.

"Oi, that was mine." I paid fifty quid for it and she had necked enough already that night.

"Sharing's caring."

I just looked at her and shook my head disapprovingly because of her drunkenness but I was also kind of happy inside that she was talking to me.

Rosemary went to grab another shot, but I grabbed them both and downed them quickly, to my detriment. I stuck out my tongue and waggled it about, trying to relieve the worst burning sensation I'd had since I got thrush by taking antibiotics for too long. Rosemary, at this point, pretty much had her head resting on the bar, looking up at me very confused by the tongue wagging. I looked at her and said, "Time to go home, I think."

She shut her eyes and tried to go to sleep.

I ordered a cab outside the bar and we both sat in the back seat when it arrived. She gave the driver her home address and then decided to go to sleep on my shoulder. I did ask her if she wanted to go and tell her friends that she was leaving, but apparently, she was well known for disappearing on nights out and not telling anyone where she was going. I didn't know that was a thing, but apparently it is.

Once we got to her house, I had to wake her up and wipe her dribble off my jumper. She groaned and I walked her to her front door, helping her find her keys on the way. I returned to the cab, waited in the back seat and watched her walk in, and then off I went home. The cab to hers wasn't necessary for me as I lived walking distance from the bar, but I wanted to make sure she got home, without bugging somebody else along the way of course. The time on my phone was 12.04am.

To cut a boring story short, unbeknown to me, one of my friends pulled one of Rosemary's friends that night and I had to listen to the gory details in the group chat for most of New Year's Day. The evening of New Year's Day, I got a text message which just read: "Thanks for last night Mr Sambuca x."

Spoiler Alert: it was Rosemary. She asked her mate to ask my mate for my number to thank me. From there, the 21st century texting back and forth romantic communication began.

I learnt about her family and that she was studying History at university. We discussed horror films, and my distain for the genre. We went through a good few days of just discussing the pitfalls of Socialism and more importantly a fearsome debate on who the best *Big Brother* winner was. I made a good case for Anthony Hutton the Geordie who fingered Makosi in the swimming pool. Rosemary made cases for Kate Lawler and Craig Phillips. After discussing the most recent winner, Brian Belo, at length, we remembered Brian Dowling won series 2 and the debate was over. We had a common favourite. It was our first real 'click' moment. Thanks Brian.

We didn't know at the time, but it was all downhill for civilian *Big Brother* from this point on, yet, all uphill for Rosemary and me, as we became boyfriend and girlfriend a few weeks later.

*****

I wake up lying on my back and feel quite disorientated for a moment. I reach my right arm out and Rosemary's not there. I jump up and turn the lights on in a panic. I rush to the toilet and she's not there; I'm still half asleep and confused and I feel this overwhelming fear in my body which is making me shake. Where is she? Where's Samuel? I run into the kitchen.

"Hello," Rosemary looks up at me and smiles.

"Hi," I breathe an exhausted breath out. Relief. The pins and needles in my hands are still lingering.

"He was hungry," Rosemary says as she caresses our son to her breast.

I have a tear in my eye and I'm confused by the moment of madness that has just happened.

"Okay," I breathe a sigh of relief again. I feel like I'm choking on the breath as it fills my lungs whilst I try to speak.

I walk back to the bedroom and get under the covers, wiping the tears from my eyes with the top of the sheets.

*****

Where was I? Oh yeah, Rosemary and I became boyfriend and girlfriend. For two years, we got to know each other more, and, in that time, obviously became aware of one another's faults. I soon learnt everything was my fault and she had nothing wrong with her. We had our first argument over a fart that I did which she said smelt like 'a corpse rotting in a bed of fish guts'. From there, we'd bicker about clothes being left on the floor, food going mouldy in the fridge, what TV show to watch and whether a bag of salt and vinegar crisps should have a green or blue packet. That was one of our bigger fights actually and we've still not come to a resolution. It was all just petty bickering though, nothing major, no punches thrown and no bruises in the mornings. We bickered and then one of us would laugh and the argument would be over. She hadn't even moved in yet and we were like a married couple. A married couple who didn't really believe in marriage. It was nice to have her around though. I liked it. I was just a dumb boy after all, and I needed a smart girl to teach me how to not live like an animal. So, when Rosemary fell pregnant unexpectedly, she officially moved in. The first time she fell pregnant that is.

When I told you about my friend who had a daughter who died not long after being born, I was talking about Rosemary. She was and is my best friend. I did, at the funeral, want to get up and shout "Fuck God's plan", but I was too busy grasping Rosemary's hand at the time. I was too busy staring at my own daughter's little white coffin trying to work out if she died because I made a mistake, so I didn't have time to get up and start degrading stupid religious rhetoric. The crippling feeling of doubt prevented the anger within me being taken out on some priest who had never wronged me. It is the only thing about the day that I don't regret; I never made a scene. I regret most things from that day, like the fact I couldn't bring myself to carry my own daughter's coffin into the church, so Gerry and some other family members did the honour. I regret not having the strength to hold my daughter for the very last time. Everybody really, looked down on me like I was some kind of child and they took control of the day and everything just went so quick and then it was over. I was left alone lying on the floor at my place, crying. I thought all the tears had gone, but, it's funny how sad a man can be when he's left alone with just his thoughts for company. Rosemary went back to stay with her parents for the night (which Gerry insisted upon), but I declined the invitation from my own mum to go home with her and my dad. As much as I love her, she's not great in a crisis and when dad was alive, he wouldn't have been able to offer much in wise advice either. I wish I had said to Rosemary that I wanted her to come back to our home and for us to cry together. Or shout, or scream, or do something more than nothing. I sat alone and I couldn't understand how something so cruel could happen to two people who didn't deserve the agony. Not that anybody deserves it, but I just knew that we didn't. I tried to find answers to questions I already knew the answers to. Could we have prevented it? No. Did we do something wrong during pregnancy? No. Was it my fault? No.

An autopsy confirmed that our daughter, Lucy, died of SIDS (Sudden Infant Death Syndrome), which is more commonly known as Cot Death. I put her to sleep on the night she died, and I remember clearly laying her down on her back in her little cot which was next to my bed. My sister bought her a little elephant teddy at the hospital when she was born and I picked it up and made some stupid noises and role-played the elephant trying to eat Lucy. Lucy wasn't amused at all; she just looked up at me like I was a bit special. I laughed at her unimpressed reaction and just put the elephant down by her feet. I got into bed and lay down, and on her way back from the toilet, Rosemary kissed Lucy good night on the forehead and then joined me under the covers. I clearly recall that I was restless that night. It had been a long week with Rosemary's labour, giving birth and me trying to get everything sorted at our place for bringing the baby home. I tossed and I turned that night, and ever since that day I always try to recall whether I heard something or should have noticed something was wrong. I didn't. I never heard a thing. Rosemary and Lucy were just fast asleep as far as I was concerned, and since the baby screamed the house down on her first night home, I was trying my hardest not to make any noise that would wake her up.

After being in and out of sleep, I decided to just get up as soon as light began to seep through the curtains. I was going to walk to the shop and get some bits in for Lucy and Rosemary. We didn't even need anything, but I just wanted to feel useful. I'll never forget looking into the cot to see my beautiful little child so blue. It seems like yesterday that I was reaching down to touch her and felt that she was hard and cold. Her hands were clinched in a fist shape. She still had this little smirk on her face. The realisation of what was happening sent a shooting pain straight to my heart. I picked her up and held her in my arms whilst walking into the kitchen and sitting down. "Please be a dream."

I kept saying it over and over and over again. "Please be a dream, please be a dream, please be a dream." I looked at Lucy one last time: "Please wake up, please."

She never.

She was gone.

I walked back into Rosemary. I looked at the love of my life and how peaceful she looked. I knew that I was about to wake her up and break her heart. She was sleeping on her side, facing the cot, and had a smile on her face like she was having the best dream ever. I was about to change her life forever, and I couldn't do it. I lay Lucy back in the cot and I walked to the kitchen and made a phone call to the ambulance service. Fifteen minutes later, they arrived, with the police. I told them I couldn't wake Rosemary up to tell her, and they said they would do it. I never saw her reaction when they woke her up; I sat in the kitchen like a coward and covered my ears as I heard the screams.

One of the police officers came in to let me know the procedure of what happens when a baby dies in these circumstances and that the ambulance would be taking Lucy to the hospital. I was free to say goodbye, either right then or at the hospital but I declined both. I told him that I didn't call straight away when I found Lucy. I told him I didn't even attempt CPR; but he informed me that it wouldn't have made a difference as it looked like she had been dead for some time. This was later confirmed by the autopsy. She died around 2am with the exact cause unknown, which never gave me any comfort as I would have been awake around that time and will forever wish I checked on her.

The police stayed for a while and walked me back into the bedroom to see Rosemary. I couldn't look her in the eye. We just sat next to each other on the edge of the bed looking at an empty cot. "I can still smell her," Rosemary said.

She had stopped crying by this point and was now an empty shell, just dazed and confused. We couldn't understand and we never will. I called Gerry soon after and he came over to pick Rosemary and I up and take us to the hospital. I couldn't look after her; I didn't know how. She wanted to say goodbye to her daughter, which I understood, but something within me just couldn't find the strength to do the same. I did, however, agree to go to the hospital to be nearby.

When Gerry arrived, he just looked at me and shook his head, like he knew that the only thing that could have come from Rosemary and I having a child was something bad. He hated the idea when he found out she was pregnant and barely spoke to me throughout the months leading up to Lucy's birth. I hated him for the way he greeted me at the door that morning. I learnt from Cheryl, years later, that the shake of the head was more of a shake in disbelief. He told her for the first time in his life, he didn't have the answers but felt like he needed to be strong for everybody involved. He apparently never wanted to show any kind of weakness towards me either because he knew that I was going to have to deal with a lot of the pain by myself. He thought if I saw him show emotion that it would somehow make things more difficult. I don't know if he was right; maybe he was.

Maybe I needed to have somebody there to cry with, or maybe I needed to have that feeling within me that I could step up and be strong. "I can deal with this, and I must," I kept saying to myself in my head. I'm not sure what or who was right. But I know I lost a lot of the person I was during the time I was healing, and he has never come back. I also know that out of all my regrets during that period, calling Gerry that day was the biggest one.

During the first few days and weeks following Lucy's death, we were bombarded with therapists and helplines to help us grieve. We both declined. A paediatrician and the two police officers who came on the day of Lucy's death also visited us for checks and to see how we were. Grief is a strange thing. It was the civil rights activist and poet Maya Angelou who said:

"When I think of death, and of late the idea has come with alarming frequency, I seem at peace with the idea that a day will dawn when I will no longer be among those living in this valley of strange humours.

I can accept the idea of my own demise, but I am unable to accept the death of anyone else. I find it impossible to let a friend or relative go into the country of no return. Disbelief becomes my close companion, and anger follows in its wake. I answer the heroic question 'Death, where is thy sting', with, 'it is here in my heart and mind and memories."

It wasn't until years after the death of Lucy that I stumbled upon this quote, but it really hit the nail on the head for how I felt at the time and how I would feel along the way on the road of grief. Lucy's death didn't just change how people treated me, but it changed the way I treated others. It instilled in me an anxiety that I had never felt before but have lived with ever since. There is no cure as far as I'm concerned and unless you've been infected by the seemingly slow death of your own soul then it's tough to explain.

I stopped caring about people. Not because I didn't care but because I feared what those feelings would lead to when something bad happened. I had always been self-aware of my own fate and accepted that one day I would have an end to my story. I wasn't and I'm still not a religious man and therefore I have always treated life as my one and only opportunity to do 'stuff'. What happened with Lucy just turned me into this person who didn't give a damn about anything. I could accept that I would die one day, and, for a long time, I wanted to. However, this new nervousness around death was a different anxiety to what I had previously felt. This anxiety was down to the fact I couldn't bear to lose someone else that I loved. So, it almost came naturally to me to treat people like I didn't care about them. I stopped seeing my sister Katie, I stopped going over to Mum and Dad's, missed out on loads of trips and nights out with friends and whilst I spent time with Rosemary, I was only there in body. I wasn't even scared about my own ability to deal with loss. I could; I knew that I was strong enough. My weakness was watching everyone else fall apart around me. Watching everybody else die inside, everyone else cry and I wasn't strong enough to keep picking up the pieces of broken people when it was breaking me doing it. I was scared to die because I hated the thought of how other people would react to it. Yet, ironically, I wanted to die so I didn't have to witness the after-effects of my family losing someone they loved.

Inevitably, I was unable to escape this reality of life. My dad got cancer two years after Lucy died and again two years after being given the all-clear. I had to face my biggest demons. My demons won. Whilst I tried my hardest to spend time at my mum's to help care for him as he came home from hospital to die, I was there less than rarely. My family were almost relieved that I was there when he died because I think that at stages, they had given up hope of me being around to say goodbye. I never showed up to his funeral, I never showed up to his wake and I haven't been to visit his grave since he died over five years ago now. Rosemary went to show her respects and came home to give me an earful about how I'd let everyone down and how my dad would have been embarrassed, but I didn't care. I had a sense of calm over my body when I knew it was all over and the decision was no longer there to be made. Plus, the repercussions of other people's thoughts and feelings could be ignored. The only thing that hit me slightly was when Rosemary told me that she was sitting alone and I should have been there with her. The thought of Rosemary sitting alone being uncomfortable, whilst in a situation which I had decided to ignore due to an event that we both went through together, made me sad. I promised myself from then on, I would try my best to be there for her in situations where she would be alone without me- if she needed me that is. Gerry's funeral was the first funeral I had been to since Lucy's which was now over ten years ago, and whilst it didn't go great, I think Rosemary deep down appreciated the fact I got up out of bed, even if it was to ruin the day.

So, this is who I've become. A glass-half-empty, pessimist of a man. I'm disinterested in most things and I don't take much seriously. Some say I'm grumpy, but I'd just say that I'm anti-pretending to be happy. I'm trying; I really am. I'm trying to be better. I'm just always ready for the worst to happen. I have to be. Trouble don't set up like rain.

CHAPTER 3

Rosemary has just posted up a photo of Samuel to Instagram with the caption '6 months old today'. She's also used nine baby emojis like people don't know that he's a baby. I'm not a huge fan of posting up photos of your children on Instagram for numerous reasons and none of the reasons have got to do with paedophiles. My first concern is that nobody really gives a damn about your dumb kid. Seriously! There are far too many people who do the baby scan photos, then a million photos of their pregnancy and before you know it, it's ten months down the line and I'm signing in to see albums titled shit like 'Baby Month 1, Album 73'. Nobody wants to see that many photos of your kid. Keep them to yourself! When did photo albums under the stairs go out of fashion? We need to bring them back so we can be spared photos of everybody's kid every time a new outfit is put on them or every time they do something, like breathe. I've had enough. I've also had enough of the fake 'baby is lying asleep on Daddy's chest whilst Daddy is asleep too' bullshit. None of those two pricks in the photo are asleep and we know it. Don't try and trick us. Babies don't sleep and parents definitely don't! Rosemary and I haven't slept for the past six months and we have not had time to set up some fake photoshoot. Too busy cleaning shit and vomit. Some of it is Samuel's too!

The second concern I have is there's a lot of babies out there who are just plain ugly. Now I'm not being mean, but if my kid was ugly, I would not be putting photos of his Elephant Man head up on the internet for everybody else to see and probably turn in to a viral social media meme. The problem is, people, are, liars. You see a photo of a damn right, cannot be denied, ugly baby. It's there. It's ugly. It's two weeks old and it's got the head of an eighty-year-old man. You know the ones; we all have friends who post up photos of their ugly kids. However, underneath the photos in the comments, what do you see? People, just out of this world, lying through their teeth. "Oh my, what a beautiful baby. Can't wait for cuddles."

Cuddles? With that thing? It looks like a Gremlin who's been fed after midnight whilst sitting in a lit-up pool. Then what happens is because these parents are getting so many nice comments, it makes them feel good and then they start posting more. So, the horrible spiral of having to look at a bunch of kids we don't want to look at continues. "Here's one of Harry hanging upside down- he's so funny."

He's not funny; he's four years old and looks like a bit of a cunt to be honest and I've had enough of looking at his gormless little face. We don't want it, but we're getting all the kids anyway. There's gormless Harry and the kid with the name like Jayden or something because the middle-class mum wants to look 'hip'.

41

There's Alfie, Tommy and kids with those kinds of names who are plonked down in front of the camera wearing the football kit of the team their dad supports with captions like 'Massive Chelsea fan' or 'Massive Spurs fan'. Oh, fuck off; the kid just got spaghetti bolognese on his face and tried to wipe it off with the plate he just ate from. He doesn't give two hoots about the football team you love; he hasn't even got a clue about where he is or what's going on. Then, there's little girls with any old first name but always with a second name added straight after like 'Rose' or 'Mae'. Evie Rose, Evie Mae, Sarah Rose, Sarah Mae. You get it. Those little bitches get on my nerves too. You know for a fact they're going to grow up to bully the girl with a less 'cute' name and I think we should just stop them now by telling them how dumb their name is and that nobody cares about them or their dumb parents. Rosemary thinks I'm being too harsh, but she'll never know the horrors of being chased around the year 2 playground by two twin girls called Evie Rose and Sarah Mae, who are trying to rub bird shit they found on a stick in your mouth for the millionth time that term. It gives me sleepless nights. I know what you're thinking, "Johnny was bullied as a child so this explains a lot."

Wrong. Going to pick Katie's son (my nephew) up from school is tough work. Especially when his classmates the gruesome twosome Evie and Sarah are about and have eaten too many sugary snacks. Katie thought it would be good practice for 'what's to come', but if being brutally attacked by children is what's to come then I won't be having anything to do with the school run. Luckily, we don't have to deal with any of this yet. Anyway, Samuel turned six months old today, I don't make him wear Queens Park Rangers football kits and he's a good-looking kid; anybody who doesn't like the photo on Rosemary's Instagram is a traitor and fool, but I'll leave him off my social media, just feels right.

I don't partake too much in social media anyway. I mainly use it to keep up with the news and to watch anti-Donald Trump accounts have nervous breakdowns every time he tweets. I don't put anything too personal up on any site really and my Facebook has basically become an old graveyard full of photos of me in my youth and 'Happy Birthday' messages which dwindle in numbers the older I get. The catalyst of my absence from Facebook is due to a group I'm in which was set up by an old work colleague of mine when we were made redundant around five years ago. The group was full of people who worked at the company over the years and after the initial sadness at losing our jobs, people soon moved on with their lives and the reminiscing over the good old days came to a halt. What then began was casual postings, up to four or five times a year, where one group member would announce an ex-work colleague's death and the

43

address of the funeral. There were a lot of crying emojis and comments of condolences but in truth it was a bit depressing. Although, when the cleaning lady Maggie, who had worked at our office since before I was born, died, there was an outpouring of grief and lovely stories about her. Kevin, who had also worked at the company since before I was born, was one of the first people to pay his respects by offering the services of his new business for free. The company he set up was a tribute acts business which Kevin plied all his redundancy money into and by all accounts, I've heard it's been a roaring success. I just found the thought of a Rod Stewart impersonator turning up to the funeral singing "wake up Maggie" over an open casket wonderfully amusing. Still not sure whether anyone took Kevin up on his offer as I didn't attend Maggie's funeral nor any of the other people who have died since we left. And that was the issue with the group. Instead of being this nice place of great memories and fun times, it became a bleak place and I realised I would be a part of it until the day came when it was my turn to get my death announcement posted up. Despite the bleakness, I can't leave the group. I think the kids these days call it 'FOMO' aka 'Fear of Missing Out' and whilst anybody who says 'FOMO' is a dick, I get it.

Another reason why I pop onto Facebook every now and again is because I might get a notification that I have a 'Friend Request'.

It usually is somebody with a very Asian or Russian name whose profile photo is a picture of their tits and a little side note which has a small number to text for more photos of these said tits. I love tits, but the thought of paying to see tits has always been a mystery to me. If it's not a profile photo of tits, it's a photo of a man who looks like he's not interested in tits but is interested in eating other humans instead. Or, it's a profile photo of an animal on an account with only one friend; it gets peculiar when it's a mutual one. Five months ago, it was a photo of a dog, a labradoodle I think they call them. The name of the profile was 'Available O'Mal'. At first, I didn't really recognise the name and spent far too long trying to stalk the profile, but it was one of those ones where you can only see the profile photo and the cover photo, and this fool only had photos of their stupid little dog posted up. I accepted the request anyway. It turned out to be Ava from the funeral - of course it did. She messaged me 'congratulations' about the birth of Samuel and sent me a photo of myself and her dancing at the funeral. Off guard, and in my drunken state, Ava's mum, Caroline, managed to take a snap from her chair which did not capture me in the best light. I had a beer in one hand (half of it down my shirt) and was twirling Ava with the other. I grinned as I wrote 'how embarrassing' back to Ava.

*****

45

Over the last five months, I've spoken to Ava via messages in the small hours of the morning on many occasions. Mainly moaning about being awake at 4am and how I have been googling tips on how to be a better parent. One night she joked that she would have expected me to have seen the film *Parenthood* with Steve Martin and got all my tips from the movie. I hadn't seen the film at the time but bought the DVD on her recommendation. As I watched, Samuel got bored and fell asleep in my arms. I loved it, but the conclusion was pretty much that everybody has issues and yours will only worsen when you have kids. That's what I got from it anyway.

The first few months of messaging each other was just idle chit-chat with back and forth cliched questions about our days. I found out that the dog in her profile photos was her pet but unfortunately it was knocked over by a car and had to be put down due to its injuries. I also found out she was a schoolteacher at a local school and that she had to change her social media name from Ava O'Malley to something the school kids wouldn't find. Why primary school kids would be on Facebook is beyond me, but apparently, they are, and they like to add their teachers. Weirdos.

Ava and I only really speak in the small hours of the morning and I often ask her how she manages to get up for work when she has been keeping me company until 6am on some occasions.

She apparently suffers with insomnia. She said talking to me helped, which led to me sending ten angry emojis in a row. What an insult! Talking to me, the most interesting man in the world, made her sleepy? She laughed and then told me she didn't mean it like that, and she meant I helped her clear her mind, which allowed her to sleep.

Ava also asked me if I had watched any French films since we met. I told her I hadn't had time and she understood but suggested that if I did get a minute to myself, I should watch a filmed called *The 400 Blows*. I quipped that it sounded like a porno, which she laughed at but then assured me it definitely wasn't. The film is actually about a Parisian boy who is struggling with the ups and downs of adolescence in the 1950s.

*****

So tonight, as I put Samuel in his cot, I fully expect to hear him cry and reckon I will have to bring him back into the living room to enjoy *The 400 Blows* with me. Until then, I wander back to the sofa alone to watch the movie. When I say alone, Ava is on the laptop messaging me to see what point in the film I'm at and to get my thoughts on it. She's watching it from her house at the same time and we have to press play at the same time too so we're on the exact same part. Watching it together but not together. I've had to rent it out on one of the TV apps for £4.99

which is a pisstake because that is the same price you can buy the DVD for. Ava, luckily for her, already has it in her collection.

Rosemary has gone out with my sister for a glass of wine or two, which knowing my sister as I do will turn into a good five bottles before anybody thinks about returning home. I'm glad Rosemary's gone out as she hasn't seen the light of day for a while, bar when we take Samuel for walks in his pram. Although her face said differently as she went to get ready, I know she was looking forward to getting dolled up and having a night out.

I'm only guessing but I get the impression that there's something wrong with Ava tonight. She's usually full of instant wit and always fully-loaded with a barrage of humorous abuse for me. Tonight, she's more sombre and not engaging. I ask her what's wrong.

"Nothing," she types almost automatically back, as if her laptop had the word ready for anything that I wrote to her.

"*I don't believe in Nothing,*" I write back, trying to sound clever but having no clue what I mean by that.

"*I know you're trying to sound clever and have no clue what you mean, but honestly, nothing is wrong.*"

Shit, she's got me. I browse the keys on my laptop to see if I can find any inspirational words amongst the QUERTY keyboard. I can't.

"*Ok,*" I write.

"*Anyway, haven't you got a baby to be looking after?*" she responds quickly again.

"*I do, and he is being looked after quite magnificently,*" I try to get the humour back into the convo.

"*I had a baby once, kind of, sort of, not really…*" Ava says.

And there goes the humour again.

"*Pardon?*" I don't really understand.

"*You asked what was wrong?*"

There's a silence both sides until Ava breaks and writes again.

"*You asked what was wrong, and I said nothing was wrong, but I lied.*"

"*Tell me what's wrong then?*"

"*It's a bit weird, but I feel like I can tell you this and you'll not think any less of me.*"

Silence from both sides, until Ava breaks first, again.

"Not that you thought anything of me, but you know. I'm just saying."

"You're being weird, just tell me what's wrong and I promise you I'll give you some really bad advice which you should definitely not follow, okay?" I write back to Ava, now slightly worried.

"Ha, okay."

I'm waiting for her to finish typing, now eager to know what's wrong. There's an anticipation in my vicinity as she continues to type. Finally, she comes back through.

"Well, you remember my ex-boyfriend I was telling you about, Damien?"

I do remember. She told me early on in our chats that she had broken up with him just before Gerry's funeral because as she put it, "He was a bit of a cunt-face."

"There was more to our relationship than I told you," Ava writes before I can respond.

I go to write back but before I can, she posts again. It's a long piece of writing. It's as if she had it ready and copied and pasted it to me from a place where she had it stored ready to find someone to show the words to.

"I found myself in a place which I swore that I would never be in. I like to think I'm a big tough girl and that I can stick up for myself. This conscious feeling I have about my own strength made everything so much tougher because I was embarrassed about asking for help for a situation I allowed to flourish. I blamed myself.

Basically, when me and Damien (who from this point onwards will only be referred to as 'Cunt-face') got together, everything was fine and it was nice. He was half Scottish and half English, and I used to go over to his parents' house because they did the best Scottish-style dinners and they loved me, which was also a bonus. The fact he still lived at home didn't bother me because even at thirty, it's almost impossible to get your own place in London these days. It started going sour when he started putting pressure on me to let him move into my flat. I wasn't ready for that commitment after only seeing him for less than a year; however, in the end, I bit the bullet and just gave in and it was all good for a while. My mum started to grow suspicious because he wasn't paying rent, and until then, those kinds of details just went over my head. I didn't ever feel like it was nice to ask him to pay half.

We got drunk one night at home and I plucked up the courage and asked him if he would be able to start paying rent as he lived at mine full-time now and from there, I just remember him dragging my arm and pulling me across the room onto the sofa where he held me down and screamed in my face. I can't even remember what he was screaming about because the fear took over. I had never been touched, in that way. I felt like I wasn't in control and nothing I could do would calm him down. The next day he apologised and blamed the drink and I, for some ridiculous reason, just let it go. Maybe it was a form of love I had for him which meant I ignored this behaviour? I don't know. Over the next few months, he just completely changed. He would instigate arguments just so he could use his strength to prove he was in control. I felt like I was walking on eggshells with him and I tried to avoid him at all costs when he was drinking alcohol. He started to put my appearance and personality down and got angry when I organised nights out with friends without him. He started accusing me of cheating and would go through my phone and emails nearly every day. I was trapped in my own house and I was frightened. As time progressed, the only person I ever saw was him. He made sure I lost contact with friends and would sit down next to me by the phone when my mum called to see how things were.

Another 6 months down the line, I found out I was pregnant. I feel sad tonight because, you told me, how you lost a child, and I allowed one to die, inside of me, because I was scared. I feel shit and weak for that decision. I went alone to a clinic in Ealing and outside there were just a ridiculous amount of religious Bible-bashers telling me how evil I was. I walked into the clinic not being able to say my own name because I was choking on my own tears. I wouldn't say the procedure hurt but it was uncomfortable, and I had to get the bus home alone because I had nobody to pick me up or be there for me. It wasn't the best day ever, let's put it like that.

Cunt-face found the after-care package I was given, and that night he pulled a knife to my throat and I genuinely thought in that moment, I was going to be killed. The irony being, as he chased me around the house trying to stab me, he was calling me a 'fucking murderer'. I managed to lock myself in a room and called the police, who arrived (after what seemed like forever) to find Cunt-face pouring petrol all over the house. They managed to taser him and arrest him. From there, his parents turned on me, threatened me in public and shouted abuse at me when things went to court. I saw in his own mother's eyes that she didn't even mean what she was saying to me but the instinct to defend her son came more naturally than believing he could do wrong. I suppose, you don't really know what anyone is capable of really, even yourself. I know I never thought I'd be able to have an abortion. I was brought up by an Irish Catholic, but surprisingly, when she found out, my mum held my hand tightly and told me I did the right thing. That meant a lot. Sometimes though, when I see what other people have gone through, I'm not sure.

Sorry for the autobiography. But you did ask."

Wow. I did ask. However, I did not expect this level of personal information being handed over to me. I feel like I have so many questions to ask her, but whether they're appropriate I'm not sure. I'm struck by her bravery and impressed by the way she articulates herself in telling the story. Blunt but real. I don't want to pry further and feel like it's probably for the best that I just reassure her.

"When I met your mum at the funeral, she struck me as a very wise woman. I don't think I could ever say that she was wrong. Mothers are always right, aren't they? I'd listen to her."

I wait, to see if that was an okay response. Did she need or want more from me?

"x," she responds.

I guess I did okay.

*****

Hangovers are a cruel consequence of having too much fun. Or, too much alcohol, depending on how you look at it. I, now in my thirties, often wish that I still had the ability of my nineteen-year-old self to get up after a night out as if it didn't ever happen.

These days, I'm either disabled from the forehead down when I wake up due to the sambuca shots and dangerous levels of double whiskeys that I consumed the night before or I am frozen due to 'The Fear'. The Fear is self-explanatory really. There is some fear, and that fear is, in no small part, down to the fact I am worried that I have done something stupid or upset somebody the night before and now I've sobered up, I can't remember. In my case, The Fear is justifiable because I usually do say something stupid or upset somebody and I must spend the majority of the next day firstly finding out what I did and secondly apologising for that thing I did.

Rosemary has woken up today after a night out with my sister, with, The Fear. She doesn't know exactly what she did, or said, but when I go into the bedroom to re-wet the cloth, she has plonked down on her face; she just keeps saying, "I did something bad."

She never. I rang my sister earlier this morning to see how the night was and she said Rosemary just let her hair down for once and was dancing and singing and drinking, a lot. They got a cab home together and apparently the only thing Rosemary should be worried about is the state of her bank balance after tapping her card so much last night, even when it was Katie's round. I was going to tell Rosemary about the phone call with my sister, so she would stop worrying about her behaviour last night;

however, Rosemary went out with MY CARD yesterday and since I checked the account balance today, I've decided to play with her.

"Rose, babe," I say annoyingly loudly as I walk into the room holding Samuel.

Rosemary hates being called two things: 'Rose' and 'Babe'.

"ROSE – my favourite flower!"

"Piss off," she snaps back, groaning through the pain of talking.

"Well, that's not nice language to use in front of your son."

She opens one eye. I'm standing there grinning whilst holding a naked Samuel.

"Johnny!" she groans angrily. "Why is he naked?"

"He just pooped himself and wanted to show you his new clean butt after Daddy washed him."

I get Samuel and start to bounce his bum up and down off Rosemary's sleepy face. He loves it, giggling and gasping for air through his laughs. Rosemary does not love it.

"Johnny, stop. I'm ill."

"Show Mummy your nice clean butt." I continue to bounce Samuel, holding him gently under the arms.

Rosemary, with her eyes closed, gently taps his butt with each bounce; she hates what's happening but doesn't want to ruin her son's enjoyment of the situation. I smile, claw Samuel back completely into my arms and end the agony for Rosemary.

"Say bye bye Mummy," I pick up Samuel's hand, and help him wave to his mum.

Rosemary waves back and then smiles as she falls back to sleep. I'll let her relax for now, but I'll be back.

Samuel's clean butt has made him sleepy, so I put him to bed and sit down to watch what every man watches on the week's day of rest. Super Sunday. If you haven't heard of Super Sunday, where have you been? It's the day where Sky Sports have two big games from the Premier League, back to back. Sometimes they may have more, but the usual set-up is they'll have a game around 1pm and then another game around 4pm and they'll advertise it like it's life or death. Because it is - unless a game like Burnley v Everton somehow manages to get the early Super Sunday slot which would mean I then go and watch some paint dry instead.

As I sit down with my pack of beers, I get a notification pop-up on my phone. It's Ava.

"I'm bored."

"I'm not," I reply.

"Why, what are you doing?" Ava asks.

"Super Sunday!"

"Bit boring."

Boring? Football? Who is this stupid woman?

"Wow, you are clueless my friend," I snap back.

"Both games have 0-0 written all over them," Ava writes back.

Okay, this has taken an unexpected turn.

"Really?" I ask, wondering what makes her think this.

"Yes, 0-0, both games. You should talk to me instead!"

"Ermmm, no thanks," I joke back.

"Bastard," she writes, with a new smiley face emoji that doesn't show up on my laptop but does on my phone. This explains all the empty small boxes she sends me.

"Joking, what shall we talk about then?" I say.

"Something less depressing than our last chat?"

"Ha, yes please. So much drama."

"What's your favourite comedy television show?" Ava asks, trying to get a conversation going.

"The Office," I don't even need to think. Gervais is a genius of our time.

"The American version, right?"

I choke on my beer and type back immediately.

"Absolutely not!"

"It's so much better."

"I repeat, absolutely not."

"SO MUCH BETTER."

"You're wrong Ava."

"I'm never wrong JOHNNY."

"We're going to have our first argument Ava if you don't stop this nonsense."

"SOOOOOOO MUCH BETTER," Ava replies; she must be trying to wind me up now, and it's working!

"The Gervais version of The Office, aka the only version worth talking about, is a complete and utter masterpiece."

"But the American version is not only funny, it also explores the relationships between human beings who work together further than the original ever did. I actually cared about all the characters, not just the main ones."

59

"I care about Brent; I care about Tim and Dawn. What more do you want?"

"The only people who say that they prefer the UK version are people who have never watched the American Version."

She's kind of got me with this one slightly as I stopped watching the American version after series 1.

"Wrong. I watched series 1, and it sucked!"

"Series 1? Is that it? It doesn't get going until the end of series 2/start of series 3!"

"The UK Office didn't even have a series 3. How much more time do you need to make an impression, especially when it had about 500 episodes per season?"

I think she's coming around to my way of thinking as she's taking a while to respond. She finally does.

"Sometimes you need more time to tell a good story. Yes, The UK Office was amazing, but did it stay with me? Did it make me think about my own life and make me resonate with the characters involved? No, it did not. I'd much rather sit in a room with Michael, Holly, Dwight, Jim, Pam, Andy, Erin, (not Toby), Angela, Kelly, Oscar, Phyllis, etc etc etc (the list is long) because I feel like I know them, and the fleeting good time I had with David, Tim and Dawn (who else is there to care about)

pales into insignificance. Not because I don't care about David and his gang but because I know Michael and his gang more and because I know them more, I feel closer to them, and always will."

"Blimey, somebody really likes the American version of The Office eh?"

"Hahaha, yes I do!"

We continue to speak about all kinds of topics including our mutual hatred for two-party politics and the voting system in general. We speak about our disproportionate fears; hers being clowns and mine being heights. We speak about our favourite places we've ever travelled to which is a quick chat on my behalf. I haven't travelled further than Palma Airport in Majorca, whereas Ava has travelled all over the world. Her stories from her travels in Bali and Australia make me jealous and kind of make me envious of how free she had been in her twenties. I go to try and explain how I had spent most of my twenties being miserable and how I feel like I wasted them, but I remember that today is only a day for happy talk and I delete the message in which I had so easily and perfectly described how I felt about missing out on so much. Maybe another time.

"What got you into teaching then?" I ask Ava.

"I just kind of stumbled into it when all else failed," she says.

61

"So, it wasn't your dream?"

"No, I don't think anybody really wants to be a teacher. I wanted to be an actress, the lead singer in a band, or anything to do with travelling whilst I worked. Teaching just came about when all those roads failed, and I needed some money."

"You shouldn't give up on your dreams though, right?" I ask, sensing that Ava isn't overly happy in her job.

"I think, dreams are unattainable. There once was a time when I felt many of the things I wanted to be or wanted to do were attainable and when they didn't come to fruition, it was more of a blow, because you realise maybe you're not good enough."

"You are good enough. I saw you dancing and singing at the funeral remember?" I say, trying to offer some positivity. I know; it's out of character for me.

"That's kind, but I was pissed and so were you."

"Well, you'll have to sing for me again someday," I type, and send before I get the chance to process the words I've written.

I feel like reading it out loud and hearing those words makes it sound like it wasn't okay to say. I've been speaking to Ava for six months now and at no point have I felt like this. Like, I'm doing something wrong.

"Maybe I will," she says.

I reach for a beer and realise they've gone warm. Lost in conversation, the whole day has gone by and both Super Sunday football matches are over. 3-1 and 6-0. What happened to the no goals Ava predicted? She was wrong, and this time there was no denying it.

*****

Growing apart from somebody that you love is one of the most painful things that life throws at you. Whether it be growing apart from family, friends, or somebody who you thought you would spend the rest of your life with. Some people, including me, would say that anybody who expects to spend their whole entire life with one other human being is naïve. Naivety, in my opinion, is the foundation of romance. Without naivety, a person can't really open themselves up to allow romance to flourish. You must have that optimistic verging on delusional mindset. Of course, there are exceptions to the rule. I don't see myself as a naïve person; if anything, I'm the opposite. I'm filled with scepticism and a mistrust in everybody I meet. Most people will meet somebody and take them at face value, believe their words and gain an opinion of them based on those words and the actions that follow. I'll more often than not greet anybody new I meet with an air of cynicism. However, this distrusting trait that I now possess hasn't stopped romance from continuing to be a part of my life. The thing is, whilst it's still a part of my life today, it's rare. Rosemary and I often seem to be like two actors standing on a theatre stage who have forgotten their lines and need a helping hand from behind the curtains to get the show going again. Our helping hand is birthdays, Valentine's Day and Christmas Day. Those days are a nod or an elbow which wake us up and remind us that we should show our feelings through the medium of gifts. The irony, however, is that by showing our affection on these days, we are reminded of the lack of affection on all the other days. By being romantic, it in turn, kills the romance.

The issue with calling out the brainwashing that we experience from young regarding love and life is that people are so brainwashed that they can't seem to snap out of it and thus are unable to doubt their very existence. It's scary to doubt yourself and others, but I think everyone should try it every now and again. Although, there are repercussions to this mental journey. Being somebody who doubts and takes time to sit back and question everything means I am somebody who people may not like to be around, especially if my observations in turn question those people's life choices.

I'm not a stranger to upsetting people due to the things that I say when I've had a few beers, but I do recall one time waking up with no regrets about an altercation I had with one of Rosemary's friends during a night out we had some years ago.

The girl's name was Becky and she took offence to the fact that I said, romance, as we know it in books and films, isn't what I find romantic. To understand Becky, you'll need to know that she fell pregnant at nineteen whilst dating a guy called Buck who she met at school and was her first and only love. The heated exchange began when I said that I didn't find anything romantic about somebody falling in love with the first boy who showed them attention, growing up to have kids with them, getting married, and then staying together until they died. I believe she took umbrage with that sentiment because she realised the only thing left for her to do in order to complete my unromantic idea of life was to die.

Look, I don't really care what people do. They can do what they like. My issue, is that certain people, usually think that they've done it right, and any other way, is wrong. They think they've got the most romantic story on earth, and in all honesty, I find pleasure in telling them that they don't. Yeah, I know you're sitting there thinking that my pleasure stinks of meanness, but I don't care. Teary-eyed, Becky shouted at me, "What about my grandparents!?" as if that was meant to mean something to me.

After her ranting emotional nonsense at me for about ten minutes, I finally understood what she meant by her "what about my grandparents?" line. She meant that her grandparents met after World War 2 when they were children, fell in love, stayed together, got married, had kids, had grandkids and were happy. She didn't mention the fact that they were both now dead, but I filled in the unhappy gaps. By giving me an example of that way of love and life working, she's suggesting that it must mean that it is romantic, and that it is the best way to do things. She's still wrong. At this point, Rosemary just looked over at me shaking her head as if to say 'let it go', but I was seven Peroni bottles deep and I felt like upsetting somebody who I disliked majorly.

I explained to Becky that whilst she had this beautiful image of her grandparents and their love, it wasn't real. It was a perspective and only one she had because her grandparents allowed her to see certain aspects of their relationship. Becky would have been a little girl growing up around them. Of course, they were only going to let her see the happy parts. They weren't going to sit her down and tell her the story about Grandma cheating on Grandad in 1967 with the milkman or how they had to spend four months apart in 1977 because trying to raise kids together was driving them up the wall. The possibility of the flaws in their marriage is endless, but you get the picture. When people's grandparents were married, initially, it wasn't out of love, it was at a time when people needed security. It might have been a love for security, or a love for security that grew into love or maybe even a fondness or love that grew because of the security, but let's not pretend that grandparents staying together in the twentieth century was some kind of beautiful love story. It was a different time, and I guarantee that if our grandparents' generation had the same opportunities as we do, then most of them would not have ended up together. We can travel the world; we can literally get up any day and go to the other side of the planet or even leave the damn planet if we wanted to badly. Women don't need men to be secure; they can work and vote and choose what they want to happen with their lives. That's more romantic to me. A woman who gets up and fucks off and goes and sees the world. Hangs her head out of a train in Sri Lanka and lets the wind blow through her hair. Lies on a beach in Indonesia and just takes photographs of the sunset. If she sleeps with twenty men along the way, even better! Congratulations on getting laid I say. I'll be more inclined to find someone attractive who has had some experience of the world and knows what she wants and what she likes. If she finds a soulmate, then good for her. I'd be more likely to believe the girl who has travelled the world when she says she has found her so-called soulmate than someone who was born in Ruislip and found her soulmate down the road. I believe that you can only know what you truly want with life when you've sat alone, far away from your normal life's distractions and thought about it. I've done a lot of that recently. People like Becky, they don't.

The reason I'm telling you all of this is because, even when you're sure that your relationship is the best way to do things, it's almost certain that your self-assessment is wrong. Becky and people of her ilk don't sit to stop and think about what they want or how they feel because they're scared that if they did, they would realise they've wasted their whole entire life going with the flow. And it's fucking tough to get out of quicksand when you're in so deep. You start to worry whether you could ever live without the person you've lived with for so long and you begin to believe it's just easier to stay. Their friends and family have become yours and vice versa and if you walk away, you're not only letting your partner go but also everything else that comes with that. It's scary to start again after being part of something for such a large proportion of your life. It's like Tom Hanks and Wilson in *Castaway* (yes, it's one of my favourite films and clearly so relatable). Tom lived with Wilson for so long that when Wilson fell into the sea, Tom didn't know what to do; he felt like he couldn't live without Wilson to the point that he risked his own life to try and save it. How many people are out their risking their own lives trying to save somebody else's? Trying to save a relationship because it might hurt somebody else if you let it drown? Wilson was a volleyball. How many of you have fallen out of love with your volleyballs and need to let them go? How many of you only hang on to your volleyball because it's kept you company for so long and you're not sure what life would be like without it? Let it go and see.

*****

"What are you doing this weekend?" Ava asks, adding on a thinking emoji.

"Nothing much planned, how about you?"

"Was wondering if you'd like to go out for the day on Sunday?"

I think for a moment and slap the palm of my hand into my forehead. I think about all I've just said and realise that I've never been good at taking my own advice. I reply to Ava.

"Sure, what's the plan?"

CHAPTER 4

"Happy Birthday to you, Happy Birthday to you."

It's Samuel's first birthday. Standing at the buffet table in the corner of our kitchen, I take a step back and sing from a distance. We don't have the biggest place and with everyone vying for some Samuel time, I watch on whilst trying not to get caught eating all the sausage rolls. Katie and her boyfriend Dan are here and have just finished dishing out a bundle of presents that cost much more than the presents that Rosemary and I bought Samuel ourselves. I'm not at all bothered by this fact, but Rosemary is. She keeps on coming up to me at the buffet table and whispering under her breath, "That's a bit much isn't it; he's only one."

I just shrug each time, which annoys her because I'm not annoyed at the same things that she gets annoyed about. My mum's here and she keeps trying to get Samuel to say "Nanny" whilst Rosemary's mum, Cheryl, is on the other side of the highchair trying to get Samuel to say "Granny". My mum thinks 'Granny' sounds old and she doesn't want to be known as the old Grandma. Cheryl thinks that 'Nanny' sounds like you're a babysitter (which wouldn't be far off the truth to be fair). My mum is much younger than Rosemary's mum as Cheryl and Gerry had Rosemary quite late on in their lives and whilst she doesn't mention it, I know my mum loves this fact. The rest of the people mooching about my home are friends of Rosemary's, whom I've met sporadically since I've been with her. Unfortunately, they're all mothers and that means that Rosemary is officially hanging around with a group of people who I've often had a hatred for. That group is 'Mothers Who Think They Know Everything'. Becky, who is running around the place trying to get her litter to behave themselves, is the leader of this group. Rosemary met Becky at work by which time Becky already had a wolfpack of children. Rosemary came home from work one day crying her eyes out because of a conversation where she offered Becky some advice about one of her children and was scoffed back at with the line 'a non-parent would say that'. Now, of course, Becky didn't know about Rosemary's past, but, regardless, her attitude is just one that makes me want to kick her down the stairs. I've had the opportunity to do that today whilst she hovered over the steps. Tempted, but I'm too pretty for prison. Anyway, what bugs me, is this idea that once you become a parent, it must mean you know everything about children and you now have an attitude that only people with children could possibly have anything relevant to say about your little sprogs and the fact they keep trying to eat coat hangers. I've been a parent to Samuel for a year now, and I literally know no more than I did before I had to look after him. I know more

71

about him, of course, but I haven't picked up any special parenting powers just because I've had to clean shit and vomit and pretend that disgusting food on the end of a spoon is a plane. This attitude that Becky and her gang have is just nonsensical. Is she suggesting that she knows more about kids than let's say doctors, nurses, therapists, teachers etc, all of whom may know a lot about how to bring up children or what's best for them but not necessarily have kids themselves? It just doesn't make much sense to me to shut down a 'non-parent' giving you some wise words because you're the one with the little brats and thus believe you have some special knowledge that others don't. Not to get bleak but some parents make their children's lives a living hell, because they just haven't got a clue about how to be a parent. Some kids are abused, mistreated and in many circumstances, killed by their parents. Lying on your back and getting spunked in by some horny goat doesn't really take much effort and isn't a magic potion to knowledge and an ability to bring up a child. I've got the exact same amount of advice for Becky as I did five years ago. One bit of advice would be to get your braindead son Jordan out into the air playing manhunt or riding a bike; something better than playing fucking computer games. Every time I look at the boy, he's got his head down in a games console or flicking through his mobile phone playing games. Go and burn down a shed or something man, what is wrong with kids these days?!

You know, you're told your whole young life to not get a girl pregnant or not to fall pregnant and if it happens these people who make the mistake (and it is a mistake at the time) are labelled 'stupid' or 'immature'. Then fifteen to twenty years down the line everything seems to reverse. Those people are now looked on as mature because they've brought up kids and the people who were smart and did what they were told are now looked at like they're the ones making mistakes or that they're immature. 30-40-year olds are now getting looked down upon like the kids who had kids because they're now apparently old and haven't had kids. People who force/expect women to have children are fucking idiots. Especially other women. You do you! It's ludicrous to look your nose down at someone living their best life childless whilst you think you're great cleaning up piss off your face. I know this is a shock to some people, but other human beings prefer to be alone and go travelling or concentrate on their careers over plucking out pieces of Lego from the big shit that their kid has just done in the plastic potty. It's kind of mental and quite frankly, society's judgemental bullshit can fuck off and die. There's no perfect way to do things, and no matter what you do, you're going to be called a loser by someone. You don't have to use the wise words of a non-parent, but just accept the advice if it's given. Unless it's from someone like Becky, because she hasn't got a clue, about anything.

Six months ago, I decided to have a day out with Ava. I know, on so many levels, it was wrong, and I've spent the last six months in a horrible limbo of not knowing how to resolve the hatred for myself in my own conscience. What's worse, is that I've continued to speak to Ava online and the day we had out was one of the best days out I've had in a long time. The most I've laughed and the most I've felt like myself.

I met Ava for breakfast in the Harrow-on-the-Hill area of London. Greeting each other, I thought, would be awkward. However, when I saw her walking towards me, she did this little hop, skip and jump thing to hurry herself up down the pavement, and when I said, "Hello Jonathan Edwards," as she eventually got to me, she laughed. She then hit me playfully and gave me a hug hello yet somehow managed to sit down on the chair outside the café in the same motion. She was sitting down before I even realised we were hugging. Basically, between my Jonathan Edwards joke and her dorky walk and hug technique, the ice was broken already.

The chat was easy going and we didn't bring up conversations we already had online. I was intrigued as to why she made me get a train so far away from home and it turned out this was the area where her mum lived. After I finished my fry up and she finished her omelette and flat white coffee, we headed to meet Ava's mum at a secret location. The secret, which was revealed after a 15-minute walk through the park, was a local Lawn Bowls Club.

"What's this?" I asked, flummoxed as to why Ava had brought me there.

"Lawn Bowls, Johnny. Also known as your new favourite day ever," Ava said whilst grabbing my arm and dragging me towards the entrance.

 As we entered the club through gates which were situated in the middle of this particularly gloomy North-West London park, it was like a different world. We were greeted by about 100 men and women all around sixty to one hundred years old. There were a few younger ones about, but the majority were pensioners. Every person was dressed in white and playing bowls on the big grass area whilst I stood watching in my jeans and light pink t-shirt looking a little out of place. Ava was wearing a pretty green and red dress, and stood out like a sore thumb, but for some reason, she still looked like she belonged. After watching for a while, I felt a tap on my back; I'd felt this tap before and smirked as I turned around to see Ava's mum,

Caroline, standing there holding two bowling balls. She was Zimmer-frame-less.

"Where's your Zimmer frame?" I asked.

"I've done my stretches Johnny, and quite honestly, I'm not going to get laid if I bring that to the club," she winked at me as she handed her bowling balls over to Ava.

I mouthed 'Wow' to Ava, who just shrugged and smiled with her mouth closed, as if she had heard that kind of thing many times before.

Ava walked off with her mum; and I, like a dear in the headlights, followed.

What proceeded was a day of learning how to play lawn bowls and a day of looking very confused as Caroline flirted her way through matches. "Your balls seem very heavy Geoffrey, do you need me to help you with them?" was the line that nearly made even Ava gag.

I winced and then threw my last bowl, or 'wood' as those who play the game call it, into the gutter. I wasn't very good, and the fact the ball was called a 'wood' just gave Caroline even more material.

The best part of the day was sitting down in the clubhouse with a beer and getting to know all the different people that Caroline spends her time with. One of the characters was a bloke called 'Jon-Jo'. He kept trying to refer to us as 'the two Johnnies' and was trying to get me to sign up to the club as a permanent member for most of the day. Telling me early doors that the club experiences four deaths a season minimum was enough to put me off, but I told him I would be back for a game soon; just so I didn't break his fragile heart. He already told me the same story, three times, about how he's had five heart attacks and nine heart operations. I could have been the person who tipped him over the edge. Instead, it was Caroline who nearly put the poor bloke into a coffin with the following joke. Whilst Jon-Jo had his arm around me telling me to look after Ava or he would haunt me when he dies, Caroline came and sat down next to us holding three glasses of wine (all for her).

"Hey, Caroline, what do you think of us?" Jon-Jo said, as he squeezed me tighter.

"What about you?" Caroline said whilst sipping her wine.

"The Two Johnnies."

Caroline then reached into her trouser pocket, pulled out a condom, and threw it down on the table next to us.

"Now you're the three Johnnies," she quipped.

I spat my beer out in shock and laughed out loud to the point other club members looked over in our direction. Ava was unmoved, but she was giggling at me laughing. Jon-Jo was wheezing next to me and had to get his asthma pump out. After he was finished pumping, he put it to my mouth and let me have a puff myself. I looked over at Ava, who smiled at me. I smiled back, but then a guilty feeling came over me and my smile turned faux.

On the way back to the train station, I thanked Ava for a fun day. She told me she enjoyed herself and that everybody loved me down the club and I was a natural with the elderly. It was this, natural, meaningless line that kind of touched me. I say it was meaningless, as it was probably just a throwaway comment, but for some reason, on the day, it hit me. It was a compliment for me, but also a nod to how my personality and me just being me, can affect others positively. They enjoyed my company; they liked being in my presence. That feels nice. For most of my adult life, I've always seemed to not do the right thing or say the right thing. If I say the right thing and do the right thing, it's not an achievement so I don't get praised or thanked. If I do the wrong thing or say the wrong thing, it's remembered, and I'm told that I've done wrong. It's been a long time since I've felt like I've done good without trying. I couldn't give two shits about people who I don't care about saying I've done wrong but the look of disappointment on the faces of those I love stays with me and I can't take it. Somebody just made me feel good about myself, and I think, making someone else feel good about who they are, is one of the most important things you can do for a person. This somebody, wasn't just anybody though. It was a girl, who was funny, kind, beautiful and a whole load of other traits you wouldn't be able to explain unless you spent time talking to her and being with her. She was loud but quiet and good with a bit of evil added on top. I've never liked paradoxes, but she was becoming one that I did like. She was becoming someone I cared about and that was scary.

As we ran towards the barriers at the train station, Ava dropped her bag which scattered her stuff across the floor. My train had just pulled up and I had run down the stairs to catch it before the doors closed. Ava, who had to grab a different train home, was struggling to pick up her belongings off the ground. The station was becoming quite busy as people rushed to catch their trains and I struggled to get passed the crowds and back up to the stairs to help Ava. Ava saw me coming and wanted to say goodbye so she left her belongings and walked towards me, hesitating between coming to me and going back to get her stuff.

"Quickly get your train," she said, as she reached me.

"Okay, thanks for a great day," I said, quickly looking back down the stairs at the train which was still there.

As I looked back towards Ava, she kissed me on my lips. I didn't kiss her back, but I lingered for a split second. She turned back to quickly grab her stuff on the floor as the crowds had passed. But when she turned around, I wouldn't have been there. I had walked down the stairs and jumped on the train. I sat down, touched my lips and ran my hand over my face, squeezing my cheeks with my fingers when my hand reached that position. The whole way home, I was an anxious mess. I was thinking about how something could have happened to Ava, and I should have waited for her or walked her home. Then I shouted at myself in my own head, "Walk her home? It wasn't a date." It was a day out with a friend, and you don't walk friends home from days out. Do you? I questioned everything. I have been for the last 6 months. Luckily, she got home. She dropped me a message around midnight that night.

"Hey, how are you?"

I didn't respond and I went to bed. In the morning, I had another message waiting for me that Ava sent before she went to sleep.

"Look, I just want to apologise for earlier at the train station. Hopefully, you had a few too many beers and have forgotten about it. If you have, also forget the following grovelling

apologetic nonsense. I was going to say that I don't know what came over me, but I do. I like talking to you, and your words make me feel safe. I fucking hate you for making me feel safe. I know you're taken, and you have a family and I know that everything I feel is just pure shit because I should not feel it. I know that you've got a kid and you're just awake when I can't sleep and that has allowed us to talk and get to know each other. I really hoped I would see you today and realise that we just got on over the internet and it wasn't anything more. I felt like sitting next to you today and laughing, was right. I know that's a problem, and by telling you, I'm making my problem your problem, and problems suck. I tried to speak to my mum about all of this and I thought she was going to slap me and tell me to stop what I'm doing. But she never. She told me to go with what my heart told me to do and she said if that didn't work just to grab you and kiss you. I told her she was crazy. Then she told me to take it from an old bird that if I didn't at least try and fight for the person that I love then I'd regret it for the rest of my life. She said, I might get a broken nose from your girlfriend, but it would be worth it if you felt the same too. I'M NOT SAYING I LOVE YOU. Or that you love me. Or that it's anything like that. My mum used the word love. But as you know, my mum, is mad. I'm just saying, I like you. It's the reason I kissed you. I'm sorry I did that, because it's inappropriate and it's not okay.

Thanks for today. Thanks for the two Johnnies and your laugh at the three Johnnies.

Thanks for being somebody I can be around and not feel fear. You're a bad dancer, but you're a good man.

Ava x"

I sighed after I read her message. I sighed that my behaviour had led Ava to gain feelings for me. I sighed because she called me 'a good man', when I didn't feel like one. A good man wouldn't be falling in love with another woman when he has a good woman at home.

*****

As Samuel's party settles down and the last few people leave, I begin to tidy up in the kitchen. Rosemary has taken Samuel from his highchair and brought him to the bedroom to get him changed for bed. I'm eating the leftover food whilst also trying to wash the dishes. Washing dishes and plates was a big no-no for me when I first got this place. They used to stack up and sit in the sink for weeks. As did the pile of clothes and clutter in the living room. The dinner table was just littered with crap that had been in my pockets over the months too. There was a selection of wristbands from different nightclubs, tissue, an abundance of copper coins and leaflets that I had accepted from people walking down the street. Now, I find washing the dishes relaxing and cathartic. Sad, but true. The dinner table is often still cluttered but Rosemary will pick my stuff up and move it to the cabinet by my side of the bed. When things go missing, she gets the blame, but she can't understand why I would suspect her of losing something of mine, although she's the only one who goes around moving things. It used to be a funny joke between us, that I couldn't put my stuff down on the dinner table because she was incapable of being able to walk past it and leave it where it was. These days, it's more irritating and our once funny loveable traits have become annoyances that we now can't stand about each other. I just don't want her to touch my stuff.

I finish the dishes and I walk to the room to find Samuel fast asleep in his cot and Rosemary fast asleep in our bed. I kiss them both on the forehead (as I try my best to do every night) and then walk into the living room to watch some late-night TV.

Late nights are the time where dreamers are most awake. I wouldn't say I'm much of a dreamer these days, but I still have the sleeping pattern of one. I find that this time of night is a time where I have my best ideas, or I have epiphanies about how life should be led and start jotting down plans of action with a pen and paper. I had a forests worth of paper scattered across my house in my younger years. Good ideas jotted down and stuck to the fridge. 'Things I'd like to do' lists written out and plastered to the walls and questions I wanted the answers to, written down and Blu-Tacked to the bathroom mirror. My current late-night antics consist of some form of alcohol, usually beer, or a Jack Daniels. I will happily sip a few drinks on my own whilst watching some kind of smokeless grill being sold on one of the shopping channels and become more and more intrigued by it as the alcohol goes down. I once bought a 'butt toner' for £14.99 whilst I was drunk because I fancied the woman who was selling the products at the time. This was before Rosemary of course. Scattered notes of genius died the day Rosemary moved in and so did butt toners. I blame her for the current sagging state of my derriere, but I suppose in the long run she did save me a few quid by banning purchases from television shopping channels. I still like to watch though, and dream of what could have been. My late nights recently have been more of a struggle with the questions in my head. I have asked myself if there is a reason why I've been staying up later and later and have tried to find the answer. Often, as most people already know, answering questions only leads to more questions and when you answer those questions, more questions come from the answers. It's the never-ending cycle of questions. I have concluded that I am up late because of a subconscious anxiety about Samuel and needing to be awake to make sure he is okay at all times. I battled with this idea for a while but looking at my little boy sleeping in his cot, I've agreed that there is potential for this theory to be correct. Looking over Samuel's cot, which is next to our bed where Rosemary sleeps alone for more hours than she doesn't, has led me to another theory. Was I spending time awake and alone because it meant I wasn't having to spend time with Rosemary? Either way, I wouldn't change what is happening right now. As I sit down and flick on the tele, the feeling I felt when Rosemary told me she was pregnant comes back to me. That was a funny day.

*****

"Johnny, Johnny," Rosemary screamed from the bathroom. She had only run out of toilet paper and called me in because obviously my job was to be toilet paper re-filler when she needed to wipe her bits. We were supposed to be going to see her dad Gerry because he had taken a turn for the worse with the cancer and Rosemary liked to be around for her mum. I remember this day because I had stood on a plug when I got out of bed and the day progressively got worse, until, well, it got Samuel.

We rocked up to Gerry and Cheryl's house around midday and for some reason, I thought it was a good idea to get a bottle of wine. Cheryl opened the door and greeted us both and I walked into the living room and put the wine down on the table which Gerry was sitting down at.

"Wine?" Gerry said whilst scrunching up his nose.

"Yeah," I sighed.

"Are you celebrating something? I'm not dead yet," he said, keeping one eye on the door so Rosemary didn't see him be mean to me.

"I thought you were," I said, tapping him on the back as I sat down on the sofa.

"You're not in my will you know," Gerry said, as if I was expecting to be.

"It's okay, I'll just marry Rosemary and get half anyway," I said without a change of expression. Switching to the sports channel from Gerry's favourite show *Dad's Army*.

"I was watching that," he barked.

"No, you weren't," I replied, not taking my eyes off the tv and ignoring Gerry's growing agitation.

"I don't like you Johnny," he said.

"Feeling's mutual Gerry," I whispered, knowing it would be the end of the exchange as I heard Cheryl and Rosemary enter the room.

"ROSEMARY!" Gerry exclaimed with excitement.

"I was just telling Johnny how nice it is to see you both," Gerry said, smiling like a lying little smiling cunt.

Rosemary bought it all of course; she loved her dad immensely and he loved her more than I've seen another man love anything before. She was everything to him. No man was ever going to be good enough for his daughter, and I definitely wasn't in his eyes.

To start the day from hell off, during dinner, Gerry started to choke on a Brussel sprout. His illness and treatment led to his body becoming weaker but trying to swallow a whole Brussel sprout was stupid for any man, let alone a man in his condition. I jumped up and tried to save the prick by using the Heimlich Manoeuvre. I got behind him and started to thrust, but he elbowed me full force in the face resulting in my nose running with blood. Choking, he wheezed out the words, "I'd rather die now then let you save me."

I sat down as if to say, "okay then" and my dislike for Brussel sprouts was suddenly gone knowing they took Gerry out of this world. I would have been happy with that ending, but Rosemary and Cheryl crying hysterical was getting annoying, so I jumped back up, grabbed him and gave him three big thrusts. The sprout popped out and went flying over on to my plate. Worst thing was that nobody saw where it went, and Cheryl really hates when guests leave food on their plates at dinner.

After dinner, we all sat down in the living room to play some Trivial Pursuit. I saw that Cheryl was becoming quite teary-eyed as we were playing and enjoying the game but nobody else seemed to notice. As it became Cheryl's turn to read a question, she broke down mid-sentence leading to Rosemary swiftly jumping up from her seat to comfort her mum. I looked over at Gerry and his head was bowed down. Although Gerry was a prick, he was usually the first person to jump up and look after Cheryl or Rosemary when they needed help, but he looked on this occasion as if he already knew that no amount of consoling would help.

Cheryl sat back in her seat and wiped away her tears then took a deep breath in. Rosemary stood next to her, holding her hand and looking down wondering why her mum broke down so badly.

"What's wrong Mum?" Rosemary said, continuing to stroke Cheryl to calm her down.

"We've had some bad news," Cheryl whispered, not being able to look any of us in the eye.

"What? Come on Mum, tell us?" Rosemary strained her voice through the incoming tears.

There was a silence in the room as Cheryl composed herself. Before she was able to speak, Gerry butted in for her. "I'm going to die," he said.

Cheryl laughed nervously.

"Well, we're all going to die Dad, but you'll be okay. You've pulled through worse than this," Rosemary quipped.

I looked up at Gerry, and whilst I hated the miserable git, I implored him in my mind to tell Rosemary he was going to be okay. I, however, had already done the maths on Cheryl's tears and Gerry's inability to look anybody in the eye as equalling a grim diagnosis.

"The cancer's spread my love. It's going to take me out of this world I'm afraid," Gerry said, looking down at his drink on the table.

"Don't be silly, you can have more chemo or…" Rosemary said, looking at her mum.

Cheryl shook her head.

"They said, I've got a year, at best," Gerry said, finally looking up to see Rosemary wiping tears from her face.

I was unmoved. I felt like I was watching something take place that I shouldn't be a part of. A father was telling his daughter that he was going to die, and I was a spectator that didn't want to be there. I didn't want to watch Rosemary cry, and I didn't want to watch this man who I had battled with for so long be diminished into this frail human being who was devoid of fight.

"I don't want you to die," Rosemary said, leaving her mum's side and walking over to her dad's.

"I'm sorry," Gerry said.

Rosemary was filled with tears and was trying her hardest to reign them back. She stood next to Gerry and took his hand.

"You can't go anywhere; do you hear me?" She kissed the top of Gerry's head and put the palm of his hand to her stomach. "You're going to be a grandad again."

Gerry squeezed Rosemary's hand and the tears from his eyes finally fell. It was the first time I had ever seen him get emotional and it made my spine shiver.

Rosemary looked over at me and mouthed the word 'sorry'. I nodded back, biting my quivering bottom lip. I had just found out I was going to be a dad again and even though I was in the room when it was announced, it wasn't me being told. It wasn't my moment. I didn't know how to take it all in to be honest.

As we left, Rosemary kissed her dad goodbye and with her mum, she walked out of the front door, stopping at the end of the front garden to have a hug. I stood with my hands in my pockets in the hallway and turned to Gerry just before I walked out.

"Max a year, eh?" I said.

"Yeah," Gerry responded, looking out towards his wife and daughter.

"That's a bit of a long time, anything could happen in a year," I mutter, swaying up and down on my tip toes.

"Yeah, it's a long time," Gerry said nodding his head.

I stopped still. I knew, in this moment, Gerry would hate nothing more than me pitying him. Part of me wanted to, but I never. I pretended to look at my non-existent watch and with a straight face for effect, said, "Maybe you could hurry it along, try and get out of here sooner; eat some sprouts when nobody's home or something."

"Or maybe, I could hang on in there, for as long as possible, to make sure you're doing the right thing by my daughter," Gerry said back without blinking.

I nodded. Both of us stony-faced. Cheryl and Rosemary looked back towards us and as they did, me and Gerry did a big fake smile and a handshake. I got in closer to him and gave him a hug as a show of love to the girls who were watching from the front gate.

"And even when I die, I'm going to haunt you every day of your life," Gerry whispered.

"Just make sure you're not there when me and Rosemary are making love in our bedroom," I whispered back.

"Oh, I'll be there Johnny. I'll be on the bed, watching you both," he devilishly quipped.

I took a step back from the hug, with a look of disgust on my face.

"That's just weird," I said, tapping Gerry on the side of his arm then turning to walk out the door. I hugged Cheryl goodbye and Rosemary and I watched her walk back to the house and close the door. I looked at Rosemary, and sighed.

"We're pregnant then?"

"Yup, we are," Rosemary said nervously.

"For fuck sake," I sighed again and shook my head.

"What?" Rosemary said, trying to gage how I felt about the situation.

"We're going to have to put up with all those 'Rosemary's Baby' jokes again," I sighed sarcastically.

"Shit, I didn't think about that," Rosemary said, whilst grinning.

She reached out her hand and I took it.

"I feel like today has just been a dream," Rosemary said, whilst opening the front garden gate.

I squeezed her hand tighter and said, "This is no dream! This is really happening!"

CHAPTER 5

It's the Monday after Samuel's first birthday and I've just finished my first day at a new job. I didn't enjoy it, but then again, I don't enjoy mundane tasks which are only created on mass for people at the bottom of companies so that the people at the top of companies can get rich without doing any of the hard work. Before you ask, I don't buy into the myth that people at the top had to start at the bottom and have worked their way up. In my experience, people at the top of companies were always destined to be there, either because they were born into a family who were well connected, born into money, or both. Also, the illusion of somebody with money who feels like they worked from the bottom just because they once worked at the bottom isn't really working your way from the actual bottom. Money can buy you most things including the best education, and I don't see many people who have been to Oxford and Cambridge having their first job on the phones at a call centre.

This call centre is taking inbound calls from customers complaining about their sheds. I don't give a fuck about their sheds, but I must pretend to care about them and then pretend like I'm going to fix their problem. Nobody in the office gives an actual damn about sheds, but for some reason, the management at the company believe that everybody's here because they want to be. Nobody wants to be here; people are here to get paid and feed their kids or save money for their actual lives. Nobody wants to work in a call centre taking call after call from customers with nothing better to do than complain. The issue is really with the management, because they can't comprehend that people don't want to work taking phone calls and have no interest in working their way up to be the people who watch the other people taking phone calls for a bit more money.

The reason the day was bad is because starting again at a dead-end job is debilitating. It's depressing to realise that you're in your thirties and haven't built a career or bought your own house. Although most people think I own my house, I don't. I rent it and I'm pretty much okay with that. Thankfully, I've never had the opportunity to be one of those clowns who do a 'we are homeowners' post, with a photo of their keys or them posing outside a house like Carol Smilie. Most of these people again, have had a helping hand from Mummy and Daddy or have been able to get a well-paid job early on in their lives through their connections to be able to afford a house. Yes, there are exceptions to the rule, but no person born into a working-class family in London is going to be able to afford to buy their own house in this day and age. Also, is getting a mortgage really 'owning' your own house? I'd say the bank owns it and now you're just renting it off them instead of some two-bob private landlord.

I've just finished going for drinks with my new work colleagues. I think up and down this country, after-work drinks are the only thing that prevents most people from jumping off the nearest bridge. It's the safe space where you can take the piss out of the people at work who everybody hates, without getting done for bullying. If you haven't been to work drinks and bitched about the person that everybody hates, well, I've got news for you. You're the person that everybody hates. Your name is probably Charlotte or Clare or Ciaran. Your name probably begins with a C is what I'm getting at. You're hated for a variety of reasons, but those reasons, in most circumstances, are always similar. You think you're amazing at everything but think so highly of yourself it's got to the point that it's now become a trait that everybody hates about you, which you can't see because you still think you're the best. You're probably either at the bottom of the food chain in the office but act like your middle management, which irritates those around you. Or, you are middle management and talk to everyone below you like they're stupid and you're the best. If you're a bloke, you're probably hated because you use your little glimpse of power to appear macho. 'Oh, look at me, I'm one level above you at work and now I think I'm the alpha-male around here'. You usually wield your 'power' to try and get new starters into bed, but everyone else quickly informs them of what a creep you are and your attempts at seduction fail miserably. You're rarely invited to work drinks, and you find yourself often trying to invite yourself to parties that somebody in the office is holding which you haven't been invited to. You're likely a massive suck-up to the top bosses and oblivious to the eye-rolling that goes on around you every time you talk. Anyway, works drinks are the best. You can let off steam, whilst getting drunk and repeat the process until you die, probably before you ever get to dip into the pension plan where most of your hard-earned cash is sitting.

I'm trying extra hard to be sociable. As the years go by, you lose contact with friends who you thought would be in your life forever. You think you'll be different, but you won't be. Whether it's due to people changing or priorities changing or just because you realise certain people are pure trash and you don't want them in your vicinity. People leave you and you leave others, and the fairy tale that the Spice Girls sold us that 'Friendship Never Ends' is proven to be nonsense. It does end.

I'm trying extra hard because I've realised that I don't have many mates. You build this big selection of human beings in your life but how many can you actually call friends? True friends. At 18 and 21, you have about 200 people at your party, at 30 you can just about get a decent amount of people together in the same room. Now on my way to 40, I'm wondering who will be on my guestlist when the time comes, and I realise that it's going be me who needs to make more of an effort to let people into my life. Obvious problem is, I don't like people.

When something tragic happens in your life, you soon see who your real friends are. They often come in surprising forms, sometimes lurking in the guise of just an acquaintance whom unbeknownst to you was capable of beautiful forms of love and support.

For me, this person was Mohammed, my newsagent. Mo is probably about 10 years older than me but acts about 20 years younger. Although he wasn't born in this country, he's been here for a very long time and he learnt early doors that in times of crisis the first medicine we go to, is humour.

You all know what I'm talking about. On 9/11, before the towers even fell, we were getting text messages with jokes. When anything bad happens - whether it is kids going missing, planes crashing, terrorism – there's jokes. I don't know whether it's a quintessentially British thing, but I get the impression that in most countries around the world if a loved one falls over in the street, family members are not lying on the floor with a stitch from laughing like they would be here. Embarrassing moments are never let go; they are brought up at family occasions for the rest of time. I once shit myself in year 2 and went the whole day telling the teacher I was fine even though she was asking me if I needed to use the toilet for about six hours. I just kept it in my pants. I walked around the whole day saying 'what's that smell' with everybody else, knowing full well I could feel the squidge in my 'Teenage Mutant Hero Turtles' pants. After school, the teacher told my mum that I had shit myself, and that is now what we talk about over Christmas dinner most years. We take the piss out of others and people take the piss out of us and that's the way it always is. I guess it's a coping mechanism: an 'if I don't laugh, I'll cry' type of situation. Whatever the reason as to why we behave the way we do, Mohammed, didn't quite get it right to begin with, but in not following the status quo, got it very right in the end.

I remember not long after Lucy passed away, I would make any excuse to get out of the house. "I'm going out to get milk," I would shout to Rosemary, knowing she wasn't listening to me. There was already milk. I used to pick up a bottle which was half-full from the fridge, take it with me outside and put it in the bin; go for a walk and then pop into Mo's to buy a new one.

Mo had owned the shop for as long as I'd lived in the area, but our relationship by this particular point, when I ventured in for some milk, had only really gone as far as me saying 'thanks boss' every time I paid for something. I didn't really know much about his life and he didn't really know much about mine. I knew, however, as soon as I walked in that he knew that my daughter had just died because his face did that sinking thing and he put his mobile phone down and pretended to look busy. He came out from behind the counter and walked along the shop floor acting like he was tidying the shelves. News travels quick around here, especially when an ambulance turns up at your house during the small hours. There's just something about emergency services being in eyesight that makes people very inquisitive isn't there?

I got my milk and wandered over to the counter where I saw Mo's phone was sitting. I looked at it and I kid you not, he had been googling 'Dead Baby Jokes'. He saw me waiting at the counter and scurried over, looking slightly nervous and slid into position to serve me, grabbing his phone back at the same time.

"Hello," he said.

"Hi."

"Just milk?"

"Yes please," I replied.

We exchanged money and just before I walked away to leave the store, he spoke again. "Oh, before you go."

He waved at me as I turned around to look at him. What do you call a baby on stick?" Mo said.

"I don't know, what do you call a baby on a stick?" I said, feeling a bit awkward but so fucking depressed I just went along with it.

"A Kebabie."

So that was it. I laughed slightly; Mo laughed with a sense of relief that I was laughing, and I didn't leave the shop for nearly three hours.

He had this dorky kindness that I needed at the time and he welcomed me in and for some reason he just spoke, and we spoke together, and it was nice. It wasn't fake sympathy and lethargic repetition of the same old rhetoric that you hear. It wasn't that Mo was incapable of understanding how to behave around grief, it was that he was trying to show his sympathies in a way that was moulded particularly for the person he was trying to express the sympathy to. I reckon he probably got to know people who walked into his store quietly for many years and could have individually tweaked his sympathies for any man or woman who walked up to his counter. On this day, he got it right, for me. I needed someone to not be scared to offend me or upset me and hearing this stupid joke that could have been a trigger to others really did make me smile. Even if the joke was crap. Trying to explain it now is difficult, but Mo definitely was a small but key ingredient to my healing process.

I remember there was a point where we laughed and then he just looked at me and said, "I'm sorry to hear about your daughter."

The laughing stopped and the smiles turned into a bow of our heads. We were sombre for a moment and then he said to me, "You know, in Islam, there's a saying…"

He then forgot what the saying was and was fumbling around his phone trying to find it.

"Okay I found it, I think this is the quote, ready?" Mohammed said, excited to tell me.

"Okay, I'm ready," I said.

"Everybody has to die," Mohammed said, then looked up at me.

I remember saying, "That's not really a good quote, that's just a fact."

"Yeah it's a bit of shit one isn't it," Mohammed said, upset that he couldn't think of anything wise to say to me.

"I'm sure I've heard a really good one, and I will find it, and I will tell you," he said.

"Okay, but just promise, you won't say none of these quotes or jokes to my girlfriend, deal?" I said to Mo.

He nodded.

In the early period of my grief, Mo was there for me and nobody else really got to see that. On one occasion, he took me out to the park and showed me this area which is secretly located behind a bench that has been dedicated to a girl who died. You can slightly push the bushes apart just behind the bench as if they were a bush-like door. It leads to this little stream and an area where you can sit on the grass. It was an unbelievably peaceful place to be during times where I needed to reflect on everything that was going on. Mo told me he used to pray there but when pressed on why he no longer prays, he changed the subject quickly. He just said, "This was my place to be at peace and now it is yours."

It was one of my regrets of that time that I was opening up to Mo, but he didn't open up to me much. I did get to know him on a better level though and he became somebody I would call a friend.

So anyway, the night with my work colleagues, is over. I'm drunk and I've reached that level where I don't want the fun to stop. Unfortunately for me and my need to carry on the party, everybody else has gone home. I'm just standing in the street with a kebab, and a phone with a dead battery. I begin to walk, drunkenly.

After a while of wondering the streets, I've got to where I was aiming for. Not my home: Ava's. I stumble up the steps and ring the buzzer. There's no answer. I ring again. No answer. I ring again and this time hold the buzzer down. After a while a sleepy voice answers, "Hello."

"Come on in. It's freezing out there; you're going to catch your death," Ava says, with a worried sound to her voice, opening the front door. I walk in and through the hallway into the living room. Ava is just wearing her nighty which has cartoon photos of baby sloths all over it. I'm slightly tipsy and can't gather whether my unexpected appearance at her door was genuinely welcomed, or she's just being nice.

"How did you remember where I lived?" she asks, as she pours me a glass of water in the kitchen which is attached to her living room.

"Errm, I just remember you telling me you lived opposite the tennis courts and then I kind of guessed your house would be the one with lots of chrysanthemums in the front garden."

"What made you think I like chrysanthemums?" Ava enquires, slightly confused, and genuinely inquisitive, as she comes and joins me on the sofa.

"It's just a bit of a pretentious flower isn't it, and you're a bit pretentious," I quip drunkenly, taking the water out of Ava's hand and gulping some down.

"Excuse me! You can't come to my home and start calling me pretentious at 1am on a weekday!"

"Should I have waited until the weekend?" I say, taking a sip of water.

"Shut up, what's pretentious about me?"

Ava grins, I think she knows I'm drunk and being naughty. I know I'm being cheeky, but I continue anyway.

"Oh gee, where do I start?" I take off my blazer and sit on the sofa.

"Don't get too comfortable, you're not staying if you carry on being a prick," Ava smirks.

"Well, let's start with the French films, that nobody has ever heard of."

"Shut up," Ava says, as she playfully kicks me in the leg. I lie back in the sofa.

"And what about folded crisps eh?" I say, putting my empty glass down on the side cabinet.

"Do you know I was at work the other day and there was somebody who didn't know what a folded crisp was? A folded crisp is literally the exact description of what it is. A crisp that has folded," Ava says.

"Your work mates sound like idiots," I say. Ava comes and sits down next to me, moving my blazer to the arm of the sofa as she does.

"They are."

We look at each other for a moment and Ava reaches out to put her hand on top of mine.

"Look," she begins to speak.

"Can you order me a taxi?" I say. Pulling my hand away from hers. A guilt-ridden sick feeling has overcome me out of nowhere.

She stands up quickly. "Sure."

The wait for the taxi is awkward. I feel drunk and Ava is sitting at her dining room table whilst I'm just sitting on the edge of the sofa waiting. I pick up my blazer and put it back on.

"I'm just going to wait outside, if that's okay," I say, standing up. I've barely been here two minutes and I'm leaving already.

Ava stands up with me, glad for the break in silence. "Yeah, sure, will you be okay out there?" she asks.

"Yeah," I nod.

I walk to the front door and open it. I go to turn around to face Ava. I want to say something. I can feel her behind me, waiting for me to turn around, but I don't. I just open the door and leave. I hear Ava close the door behind me.

I finally get home, having spent the taxi journey contemplating so much. I'm not the best at trying to discuss feelings in person, so I begin to write a message instead.

Ava,

I know you're probably asleep right now and won't be able to reply to me. I'm sorry that I turned up at yours like a drunken fool and spoke a lot of crap.

I was trying to rack my brains in the taxi home as to why I felt the need to come and see you and hang out, but in all honestly, I didn't need to think for long. It's not a thought thing with you - it's more of a feeling thing. This worries me. The fact that it feels good to be around you is worrying. The fact that I don't need to think whether I'm doing or saying the right or wrong thing around you and can just say and do what I feel at the time is a peaceful feeling that I haven't felt for a long time.

I don't want this to come across as anything negative to do with my relationship with Rosemary. Maybe by mentioning her at all, it will inadvertently give you the impression that my fondness for you is because of something wrong with her. There's nothing wrong with her. I love and care for her more deeply than I ever have. I love her more now than I did before I knew you because you have made realise that I have the ability to care for another; that ability scares me. It scares me because my ability to care and feel for you is also the ability to hurt somebody I love. I cannot hurt Rosemary; she has hurt too much in her lifetime. I cannot break what is left of her heart.

I'm self-aware enough to know that what I feel for you is wrong. I can't exactly say what these feelings are, mainly because by writing them down I admit them completely to myself and the conscious denial I'm partaking in is the only thing that is keeping me from a brink I feel I could not come back from.

I pause for a moment and take a deep breath in through my nose, then a big breath out through my mouth. I look around the room. I'm trying to find inspiration or a sign to find the right words. I know what I want to say but I feel like I'm just ranting on about nothing. I press send anyway. Now it's time for bed.

*****

Rosemary and I are both sitting in our living room. It's long been the case that we rarely share the same sofa and what was once quite a touchy-feely relationship has become one where having our own space is being able to breathe. I'm sad that this is what we have become. Being near Rosemary once helped with any anxieties that I was feeling but now the anxiety is coming home and having to sit in the same room and look at her face. She looks miserable, bored, uninterested and frustrated. But she doesn't speak; she just sits there, looking as she does. That creates such a burst of anger within me that I want to let out, but I don't. I want to scream at her and tell her that her miserable behaviour is making me miserable, but I can't. Because I know how she feels, and I know when you're so hurt by life, you can't pretend to be anything but sad.

This is something that I've always feared though. Sitting in a room with somebody I love but still being lonely. I've heard about this feeling before, but you can't really appreciate it until you can feel your heart weeping. I actually imagine my heart having eyes and the eyes welling up and trying really hard to stay strong, so the tears never fall. They do fall though, and they sting. They sting my insides like I've swallowed a wasp. Some might say 'if you're not happy why don't you just leave', but that's too simplistic. It's not about not feeling happiness, it's about feeling nothingness. It's short conversations; it's walking past each other as if we aren't even there; it's going to bed and falling asleep alone in an empty room or waiting for one of you to fall asleep before the other gets into bed. I have so many questions and yet again, none of the answers. Am I falling out of love? Or am I falling into hate or indifference? I look up from my phone to the TV and see Rosemary still peering down at her phone. She's got her legs curled up to one side and her hair scrunched up in a bun with no make-up on. She wears just her pyjama top and shorts and as she itches her leg, I can almost hear her nails scratch through the spikey hairs poking up. We still have this comfortability between each other in some ways but then it's uncomfortable in other ways. It's like we're comfortable with the uncomfortableness, and in my view, that's just indifference, and indifference is worse than hate. I feel at times that I do hate her and then in other moments, I feel like I can't even be bothered to hate her. It's too exhausting.

We've been comfortable with each other since very early on in our relationship journey. I remember when we went to one of my friend's house parties one night and Rosemary was sitting on my lap when she looked down and noticed that she had come on her period. My white top had some blood on it, and we were in a packed room with everybody talking. I just picked her up and wrapped her legs around me, so the blood was covered, and I carried her into the bathroom. Everybody was chanting and singing thinking we were going in there to have sex, but it was a bit more intimate than that. Rosemary was panicking, whispering to me, "What am I going to do?"

But, I had already thought of a plan. I banged my fist against the door and shouted "ouch" very loudly so everybody could hear. I took off my t-shirt and put it to my nose and walked out to lots of laughing and jeering sounds. "I've got a nosebleed," I announced to the room.

The laughing got louder as I walked over to grab Rosemary's bag which I brought back to the bathroom and handed to her so she could get a sanitary towel (I knew they were in there as I saw them many times when she was rummaging around). Rosemary was very embarrassed, but it didn't faze me at all. I grew up in a house which was mainly just me and two women as my dad was always working, so I knew the ropes when it came to that time of the month.

I think I'm becoming everyone I despise. People who settle and people who just never have the strength to step out of their comfort zone and do what they want. I'm only in my 30s and I feel like I don't want to spend my whole entire life in this environment, yet my feelings don't seem to be important to me. If I lose Rosemary, I lose everything I've known for over a decade. It then sets up a life where there's a possibility another man will be living with my son and influencing his life. My hate for that idea is stronger than my need to be happy. My fear of a change I don't want is stronger than the strength I have to pick myself up and look for the change I do want.

I put my phone down and I get up out of my seat. As I walk out of the room, I can feel Rosemary's head turn to watch me. I'm just wearing my shorts and a t-shirt and although I know it's going to be cold outside, I just need to get out of this house. I feel claustrophobic and I feel like the walls are caving in on me. I open the front door and I walk down the stairs quickly. I open the door at the bottom of the stairs which leads to the street and I walk out on to the pavement. It's cold on my bare feet. I take a few steps towards the road and bend forward, leaning on my knees with the palm of my hands, taking a deep breath in as I do so. The cold air is refreshing, and it fills my lungs. I look around at the streets that I've walked out to every day for the most important days in my life. I watch the light from the streetlamp flicker over my head and I begin to walk across the road. "Johnny, please come back," I hear from behind me.

I stop and turn to see Rosemary on the pavement; then, the light gets brighter.

CHAPTER 6

Where the fuck am I? I can't keep my eyes open for more than a second because I'm blinded by the lights. I'm now singing, *"How did he not find the baggy, with his hand in my shoe? Way too close for me, oh well at least they allowed me through. Should be a good night in here, Ramo in the main room. People keep pushing me though, no reception on the phone. And I'm thinking."*

Ironic that it's The Streets song I'm singing in my head, when standing on the street was the last thing I vaguely remember. I open my eyes again and try to keep them open for longer. I look down at my arms and notice I've got more needles stuck into me than Mark Renton. Another hazy memory comes back. Rosemary calling out for me from the pavement. Is she okay? I feel sick. My stomach hurts and my head is pounding. Actually, everything hurts. Exhausted, I close my eyes again.

After falling back into a deep sleep and dreaming about a snake crawling on me and trying to have relations with me, I forced myself to wake up again. I've often had lucid dreams in my life, and I seem to have an ability to control the dream because I am somehow conscious of what's going on and can control the me in the dream to do something which makes the real me wake up.

I don't know what the snake dream means, but I had enough of it when it was trying to get in my arse. Please note, this is nothing against my gay bredrins. I'm very pro-be-who-you-are. It's one of the reasons why Rosemary and I never got Samuel baptised. How could we in all good conscience baptise our kid in a church, to a religion, which would turn its back on our kid if they grew up to be gay? Why would any parent bring their child up in a religion if that religion could one day turn around and tell your child that their love is wrong and is not as worthy as a heterosexual love? Yeah, it's a big 'what if' but the way I see it is that a religion should be honoured to have my boy be part of it, not my boy be honoured to be part of it. Look, I'm rambling, the snake in the bum dream is not anti-gay. If I loved another man and he wanted to go in the bum, I'm cool with it. I just don't want some random snake in a nightmare crawling in my butt, simple as that.

I look around the hospital room and there's a few balloons' and 'get well soon' cards scattered across a table in the corner. The first thing I notice is that I can't feel my legs. For fuck sake, I'm going to have get fake ones, aren't I? I'm going to have to be a Paralympian and go on The Last Leg and make jokes about being disabled. This is what my life is now. I peel back the covers slowly; my legs are still there. I try to wiggle my toes; I can feel movement and when I look down towards the end of the

114

bed, I can see them wiggling. My head rests back on the pillow in relief. I'd rather have my legs than be on an advert calling myself 'superhuman' like I'm one of the X-Men. I had a friend at school called Sebastian who was in a wheelchair because he had lost his legs at birth and he nearly committed suicide. Not because he was upset about not having legs, but due to people who kept on patronising him about how brave and amazing he was. Applauding him because he wheeled himself to the toilet and managed to get onto the toilet and back into his wheelchair without rolling in his own shit. He was just a normal kid like me apart from the fact he had no legs. Yet the constant praise for doing normal things that he could do normally led him to nearly wheeling himself off a cliff. He used to say to me, "Oscar doesn't have any eyebrows, but nobody treats him like they do me."

Oscar was a kid who joined in year 9 after coming to England from Sweden and had had the unfortunate disability of being very very blonde. He was so blonde, it looked like he had no eyebrows. People fancied him though, so, go figure.

*****

I'm getting irritated. I'm too stiff to be able to move and nobody seems to be coming into this room to check on me. My mouth is dry, and I need a drink, plus I think I've pissed myself four times since being awake. Then out of the corner of my eye, I see Rosemary in the hallway talking to a nurse. As she finishes the chat, she walks towards the room I'm lying in and opens the door. She walks over to the bed and peers over me.

"Hi," she says.

"Hi," I whisper, I don't have the strength to say much more, but I try.

"What happened to me?"

Rosemary takes her jacket off and puts it on the back of a chair that she drags over to the bed. She sits down and rests her hands on my side.

"You were run over by a car," she says.

I feel a bit weak again, and I close my eyes.

As soon as I do, I'm in a lucid dream. I'm standing in the road again, looking at Rosemary asking me to come back to the flat. As I walk towards her, I'm hit by a car; it was speeding and screeches to a halt at the end of the road. As Rosemary comes towards me to help, I open my eyes, and as I lay on the floor, I see somebody get out of the car that just hit me. It's Ava. She's shaking, and bleeding. I feel like I need to get up to help her, but I can't. Why was she speeding and near my house? I ask myself this in the dream. Then from behind her, her abusive ex-boyfriend appears like a shadow figure. I feel it's him rather than seeing an actual person. It's one of those dreams where it's the feeling that scares you, not what you're seeing. I can feel myself slightly waking up, but I can see Ava being led away, further and further away from me. I turn to Rosemary for help, but I can't speak because I'm hurt. Wake up, wake up, wake up!

I wake up again, and I'm panicking, in real life.

"What happened?" I ask Rosemary.

"You stopped in the road, a car was travelling down passed ours and he just hit you full force," she says.

"He?"

"Yeah, he was a young lad; he was quite shaken up but he's fine," Rosemary says.

He's fine? I think to myself. What about me? I thought I lost my legs. What the fuck is going on?

"You were crossing the road, then when you heard me call, you stepped back into the traffic and it was almost impossible to miss you," Rosemary says.

"Okay," I say, accepting her story, too tired to ask any more questions.

"You've been in an induced coma for three weeks due to the swelling on your brain, but the nurses and doctors think after a bit of physio you'll make a full recovery."

"Wow," I say, shocked at the fact I've been in a coma.

"Apparently you've been waking up on and off today, so the nurse gave me a call this morning to let me know to come in," Rosemary says, looking sombre and tired.

"I don't remember," I say, looking at her for more answers.

"It's okay," she says.

I go to talk but before I can get the words out, Rosemary speaks again.

"Look, I was going to wait until you were up on your feet, but it's been three weeks and I need to say something to you," Rosemary says, with a tear in her eye.

"What?" I ask, scared. "Where's Samuel, Rosemary?"

"He's fine," she says quickly. "Just listen."

There's a moment of silence as Rosemary shuffles closer to the bed. She's emotional and she looks like she's holding her tears in. She looks up at me.

"When you were run over, I didn't know what to do. I panicked, and I screamed, and nobody came. I ran back into the house to call an ambulance, but I couldn't find my phone, so I picked up yours and rang 999. I went back outside and I lay next to you on the road until the police and ambulance got there. I thought you were already dead. As I sat right here by your side three weeks ago, your phone kept getting messages, and I was thinking it could be important so I thought I'd look so I could let the person know what happened. A week later, I still couldn't bring myself to tell this person you were here, and that you could die. I spent a week reading the messages from you and her over and over again. The messages kept on coming and I realised that this person, was somebody who cared for you and I made the decision to let them know. I let her know."

"Rose…" I try to speak. Heart sunk, tears in my eyes.

"No, Johnny. I let her know and she came here. She was scared, like I'm sure you are now, but she came. She said she had to. Because she loved you."

Rosemary wipes the tears falling down her face. Watching her trying to compose herself is killing me. She's shaking and biting her top lip with her bottom teeth, trying to say what's on her mind but being in pain with every word.

"She's nice and I know this because we went for coffee at the hospital cafeteria. We spoke, and we cried. I've got to know her a bit and I can see why you like her."

"I'm sorry." It's not good enough, but I say it anyway.

"I'm angry with you Johnny; I don't hate you."

There's a knock at the door. I expect it's one of the nurses.

"Come in," Rosemary says, not taking her eyes off me.

I look towards the door.

It's Ava. She's holding Samuel. She walks forward slowly towards the bed. I mouth "Hi" as she reaches me and she mouths it back.

"Hello Samuel," I say, as Ava lowers him down so I can hold his hand.

"Say hello to Daddy," Ava says.

"Daddy," Samuel mutters, sticking his dummy back in his mouth afterwards.

"What? He can speak?" I look at Rosemary for answers.

Rosemary nods. "Apparently so."

"Yeah, I've been looking after him a bit this month and we've been practising," Ava says.

I look at Rosemary again, she forces a smile.

"What about Mummy?" I ask.

"Not yet," Rosemary says. She waits for a moment then stands up. "We'll leave you two to talk," she says with her back to me. Ava hands over Samuel and he is carried out of the room by Rosemary.

"Rosemary...Rose..." I try to call out, but she doesn't hear. Or if she has, she doesn't acknowledge me.

As I try to wake myself up from this dream, Ava sits by my bed. She grabs my hand and squeezes it. She squeezes it hard, and I realise that this is real, and I don't know what to think or feel. I look at her and after a moment, I squeeze her hand back.

"This is weird," I say, still holding her hand.

"I know," she says, looking down at our hands intertwined.

"It's okay though, everybody just wants you to get better."

"I'm thirsty," I manage to get out, choking on my own dry mouth.

Ava reaches over to the water on a small cabinet next to the bed and pours me some into a small paper cup. She leans over me gently and drops a small amount into my mouth.

"Thanks."

Ava sits back down. As she does, she reaches out to hold my hand again.

"What the hell's going on?" I say, still very confused.

"A lot of stuff has happened, since you've been here," Ava says. "I know, it's going to be weird, it's still weird for me to be honest."

Ava looks nervous. Like she's unsure of whether I want her by my side. I don't know what to think or feel to tell you the truth. I'm glad to see her but I need to sort things with Rosemary. This whole 'waking up to my life being changed' thing is giving me a bigger headache than when my actual head slammed off the pavement. Instead of waking up to an abundance of gifts, flattering social media posts about how great I am and a newfound love for life; I've woken up in the film *Gregory's 2 Girls*.

"I need to speak to Rosemary," I say, noticing Ava pull her hand slowly away from me as she hears the words.

"Right, okay, sure, I'll go and get her," Ava says, nervously getting up at the same time. She looks lost. I feel sad for her in my heart straight away because I can see that she thinks I don't want her here. That's not the case; I just need to speak to Rosemary.

I hear the door close behind Ava as she walks away. Moments later, I hear it open again as Rosemary enters and walks towards the bed. She stands over me and looks down. I stare back up at her, neither of us say anything, until the silence hurts too much, and I have to speak.

"What's gone on?"

Rosemary shakes her head.

"I don't know what to say to you Johnny. Well, I thought I didn't. But I've written you a letter and hopefully it fills in the missing pieces to things you need to know," Rosemary says whilst taking out an envelope from her jacket pocket and laying it gently down on top of the bed sheets.

I swallow hard, trying to catch a breath. "I didn't mean to hurt you," I say, knowing it's not good enough but wanting to say something anyway.

Rosemary composes herself; she uses both her hands to wipe her eyes at the same time. She sighs heavily and looks at me closely.

123

"You know, for the first week when it was touch and go and I was here alone, I was praying to a god I don't believe in, begging them to let you be okay."

I reach out my hand, she ignores me.

"Every part of me thought I was going to lose you in this room," Rosemary says with a tear in her eye. "And eventually I was right."

She turns around and walks slowly towards the door. She stops for a moment as if she's forgotten something else she wanted to say. But then I watch her leave, never looking back.

Tired and confused, my head hits the pillow. I feel like I sleep for a minute, only to be woken again when I hear the door re-open. I look up expecting to see Rosemary return, but it's a nurse.

She walks up to me and checks some of the machines that I'm hooked up to and helps me have some more of my water.

"Is that woman who just left gone?" I ask.

"She's not gone; she's outside," says the nurse.

Thank fuck. I can't leave it with Rosemary like this.

"She's been outside for most of every day for the past two weeks," the nurse says, walking back over to the door of the room. She opens the door. Ava is standing there, in the corridor.

"He wants to see you," says the nurse to Ava.

Ava walks in. She stands by the door as the nurse closes it behind her.

Ava waves at me as if I'm very far away.

I wave back.

*****

Two weeks later and I'm sitting in a physiotherapist's waiting room. Being bedridden for all that time means my body isn't in quite the nick it should be, and I'm being made to stretch and exercise more these days than I've done in my whole entire life. I've never been able to touch my toes and the dirty looks the therapist has been giving me on my last few visits because I can't even touch my knees are now quite off putting. I just thought it would be massages and nice smelling oils being rubbed into me. Not on your nelly! It's been hell. I've been manipulated and contorted into positions that a normal man should never be able to bend into. It's been giving me more pain than soothing the pain I'm in, and I've just had about enough of it to be honest. I just want to rot in my bed with meal deals and sweets whilst watching the latest murderer documentary on Netflix.

I keep on having to get the bus too. Katie is angry with me and Mum doesn't have a licence anymore. Mo from the corner shop offered me a lift but his breath smelt of whiskey this morning and I heard him drunk in the street singing 'Sweet Caroline' by Neil Diamond at 4am. He started changing the lyrics to 'Sweet Kharian' which is the city in Pakistan where he was born and his family still live. Mo reckons he's got ADHD but when he was younger instead of getting checked out, he was told to just pray to Allah. Allah never answered his prayers, so now he just describes himself as 'hyper' and 'coked off his tits'. He always just shows me a can of cola from behind the counter every time he makes that same bad joke. He also always smirks because he finds it funny, every time. Mo is a nice guy and sometimes it's nice to have someone nearby who will always be there to not only talk, but to make you realise that whilst other things in life change, some are still the same.

I've asked Ava for just a little bit of space whilst I get used to my life after the accident. I came home from the hospital to an empty house because Rosemary has gone to live with her mum. A note was on the table saying 'Any time you want to see Samuel, we'll be at my mum's' but for some reason I feel too embarrassed to look my son in the eye. He doesn't understand what's going on and probably never will, but I just can't bring myself to be near him. I call him every day though and he listens to my voice down the phone and I hear him say all the new words he's learning. The envelope that Rosemary left for me at the hospital hasn't been opened and is sitting next to a pile of unopened letters in the kitchen. It's frustrating how life goes on even when you feel like it has stopped. The bills still need to be paid and gosh don't the companies you owe let you know about it!

Ava said she understood, but I'm not sure she did. She still messages me every day asking me how I am and if I need anything. I know it's nice of her to care but I have this anxiousness about accepting her care, like, is it acceptable? I know it's too late, but I don't want to be inconsiderate to Rosemary's feelings. I don't want to be a dick to Ava either, but I don't think it'll be okay to just continue to talk to her and be with her as I was before. It almost feels weirdly like it's even more inappropriate now when Rosemary knows about us than when she didn't. It's like I'm going to be a dick to someone regardless of how hard I try to not be a dick.

The truth is, I obviously need a break. I've woken up to these same walls every day for too long and they now only remind me of misery. I'm very unhappy. I'm not afraid to admit that the feeling I'm currently experiencing is sadness, as I've felt it before, and I know the worst thing you can do is pretend not to acknowledge its existence. You must face it and you must fight it. This becomes more difficult with each battle, because when you think your demons have been defeated, they show up again. Even when you think the sadness is gone. The rule to this with no exceptions is that sadness is never gone. It's just hiding; it's just waiting for you to be at your weakest so it can remind you that it still wants to take your soul.

Do you remember in *Back to the Future 2* they start the movie with the scene which is the last scene in *Back to the Future 1*? Well they did, but the difference was that in *Back to the Future 2*, they replaced the actress who played Jenny, so they had to redo the whole scene again, shot for shot with Elizabeth Shue who replaced Claudia Wells in the role. I feel like metaphorically you're not going to get a much better example of where I'm currently at in my life. I've seemingly replaced Rosemary with Ava, but I also feel like I'm going to have to do the scenes I've already been in again. I'm basically Michael J. Fox.

What I'm trying to say, and not very well, is that I've been there and I've done that long-term relationship thing. I feel like by starting another one from scratch, I have to do all the things that come with long-term relationships over again and if the outcome is just this bleak misery then I don't want to do it. The only positive I can take from this whole situation is that Elizabeth Shue was an excellent replacement and *Back to the Future* is the best trilogy of all time. So maybe things could work out. Maybe, I'm just being a pussy; maybe, I'm not brave enough to dive back into caring about somebody. I know what you're thinking, but...nobody calls me chicken!

CHAPTER 7

It's been a few months since I had my mini break down about life. I've spent some time with Samuel, and I've been venturing out of the house to spend time with Ava. It's helped me to be distracted. I'm still under observation with the hospital but I only have to go in to see them every 6 months now and report in if I'm feeling certain things on a list of certain feelings that they gave me before I was discharged. I'm feeling a lot of things and feelings currently, but luckily, none of them are life-threatening.

I spoke to Rosemary when I dropped off Samuel last night to let her know that I was going away for around 6 weeks and she seemed to not be intrigued in the slightest. She told me she was going away to clear her head soon too, which I was pleased to hear about. I've sat and tried to face my demons whilst surrounded by demons and it doesn't work that well. Sometimes getting away is the best thing to do and despite everything, I obviously still want the best for Rosemary.

Though our time together has been limited, I've taken Ava up on her offer to travel with her to Australia during the school summer holidays. I've been off work sick for a while now, and although I'm not entitled to company sick pay as I wasn't working at the company long enough before the accident, I do get a little bit of income a month which has kept the rent going. What I don't have the money for is a trip to the other side of the world for six weeks, but to my surprise, Ava offered to pay for my flight. I don't know why, I don't know how, but she did, and after debating it in my head for some time, I agreed to go.

We're not travelling around Australia; Ava's made it clear that she hasn't got the money for that. She has rented out a home for us to live in, in a seaside town called Lorne. Ava wants to write a book and she has said that her friends told her that the views and peacefulness of Lorne would be perfect inspiration. Lorne is in Victoria which means we'll be flying into Melbourne airport and catching a coach from there. I'm not the best at flying, but after nearly being killed by a car outside your house, it gives you a little perspective on things. I'm currently finishing the last of my packing, and as I fold up my fourteenth pair of Primark boxers, I receive a text from Ava.

"Hi Johnny.

Just a few rules for you on this trip.

1) No arguing

2) No stressing

3) No listening to Westlife for the entire plane journey. You have to pay me attention. Haha!

I've bought you a stress notepad, so every time you want to argue with someone or are getting stressed, you have to stop yourself, and write it down. Deal?"

"Deal!" I text back. Smiling as I write my reply.

I feel like every message Ava sends me is for my own good. She doesn't send me funny messages with a list of rules, or ideas that make her feel good or are for her benefit. They're always to make me happy. She's selfless and kind and humorous with everything she says and does. Despite having her own issues, she's always helping me take steps forward. It's weird to have someone like that in your life, where you can actually feel that they care about you. It's nice.

As I finish packing, I pick up the letter that Rosemary left me in the hospital. I've not read it yet and I don't think I want to read the pain in her words or feel her hatred for me in something she wrote many months ago. For some reason though, I put it in my suitcase. I hear the doorbell go; I look out of the window and see that Ava has arrived in the taxi. She waves up at me excitedly. I look around at my messy flat, dark and dingey. It's changed. I walk out of the door.

*****

I have a very low tolerance for idiots. On the flight, I unfortunately encountered a selection of idiots, but because I'm on a 'stress ban', I was unable to confront the idiots and let them know that they were behaving like idiots. Idiocy is a disease and it can plague anyone; it doesn't discriminate. Some of the least educated people I know are not idiots. This would be a good example of how lack of education doesn't mean you're stupid. On the other hand, we have MPs in Britain who were most likely given the best education, who are absolutely top of the idiocy table. Some people behave like idiots on purpose, knowingly. Then, you have brainwashed idiots and they are the ones you just have to pity. To cut a long story short, there's a lot of different idiots out there.

The idiots on this occasion were a middle-aged white man and a black family. 'Why is their age and race relevant?' I hear you say. Well, we'll get on to that. I'll set the scene. The black family were discussing Will Young at length. They were discussing the first series of Pop Idol when Gareth Gates was the clear favourite going into the final but was beaten on the night by Will in a shock result. I personally felt that Will was a deserving winner and has gone on to release some absolute classics but that's neither here nor there. Whilst the discussion started off pleasantly enough, it soon started to get stupid. One of the older siblings from the family who was in his late twenties made a homophobic comment which was met with a chorus of laughs from the rest of the family. The quite openly homophobic chat continued when the dad piped up with, "It's Adam and Eve not Adam and Steve."

Oh, yeah, that old classic witty line, often said by homophobic idiots of a religious persuasion. How do you know Adam and Eve weren't gay? How do you know Eve wasn't a lesbian? I think the serpent who deceives Eve into eating fruit from the forbidden tree is a metaphor for a woman who seduced Eve and Eve ate her vagina. I sat back in my seat nearly foaming at the mouth, but I was resolute. I remembered the ban on arguments but listening to this and ignoring it was causing me more stress than being in an argument would ever cause. I go to lean forward but Ava put her arm across me to stop me. Instead, she popped her head through the seats and said,

"Oi, do you want to keep your bigoted views to yourselves because people want to enjoy their flight without having to listen to you talking crap."

The plane went silent, people were looking over. Then the white middle-aged man leant across the aisle and tapped the idiot son on the shoulder and said, "Don't worry about her, you can't have an opinion these days; it's PC gone mad."

134

Ava turned to face the man. "Oi, Dickhead. It's not PC gone mad to tell people who think that being gay is wrong to fuck off with their bigoted nonsense."

"Politically correct rubbish; we're allowed to have our views," the bloke piped up again.

"Are you deaf? Having the view that being gay is wrong, isn't an opinion, because being gay is natural and normal and that is a damn fact, regardless of what you think or your fucking God thinks," Ava burst back, her accent turning slightly into a little London rude girl out of nowhere. I was scared and aroused at the same time. I thought she was Tulisa from N-Dubz in disguise.

There was a slight pause but then as Ava calmed down, she riled herself up in her head and kicked off again, her normal voice returning. "Opinions can be wrong you know. It would be like you telling me we're currently in a plane and me telling you that we're in a helicopter and that's my opinion and there's nothing you can do about it. I'm just going to keep saying we're in a helicopter, regardless of facts."

The man looked over at her confused but silenced.

Ava kneeled up on her seat and looked directly down on the father of the family in front of us. His shiny bald head resting on the head rest, shocked, mute and now clearly embarrassed.

"Also, Dad, the male G spot is in the arsehole, and I hear it's quite pleasurable. Which is why although I want to shove this shoehorn up your arse, I won't, because it will bring you too much enjoyment."

The man leant his head backwards and looked up to see Ava waving her shoehorn about. She gave him a knowing glare. She bought a shoehorn in the departure lounge because it had her name on it and whilst she didn't actually need one, I believe fate somehow conspired to make it 100% necessary for her to have the shoehorn in this very moment to look as intimidating as she did when twirling it about above the homophobic bloke's head.

Ava began to sit back down; as she did, she looked at the son and said, "It's often blokes who are very insecure about their own sexuality who are the biggest homophobes because they worry about their own ability to enjoy gay sex. I'd remember that next time you're making jokes about gay people. The ladies might think it's a self-defence thing. Oh and also homophobia isn't very attractive anyway, okay darling?"

The lad gulped and lay back in his seat sulking.

I somehow managed to slide all the way down my seat from cringing but as Ava sat back down, the passengers around us applauded in unison. Then, to our surprise, one of the flight attendants who was camper than a row of tents came over with a big bottle of posh champagne. "Thank you," he said, as he placed it on Ava's lap. She smiled and nodded. Breathing heavily.

I got out my 'stress notepad' that Ava bought me and opened the first page. I scribbled some quick words inside. *'Just because you've been oppressed doesn't mean you cannot also be an oppressor.'*
It often angers me when I see people whose own heritage has a history of great inequality and lack of human rights show the same ignorance towards another section of society who also struggle today to live their lives with the basic freedoms that we all take for granted. Sad really. And as for the middle-aged white fella, thanks for living up to the negative tropes that negatively affect people's dads and grandads who aren't ignorant idiots. Tropes which not too long from now, will impact me. I don't want to be judged because a very small minority of people who share my skin colour and share a similar amount of wrinkles, say dumb shit.

Anyway, we eventually arrived in Lorne, tired but stress-free. Whilst my anxiety about the journey had diminished since landing, my anxiety about my life in general was niggling away at me. It wasn't anything huge, but I just had this sense of nervousness within me. I think it had to do with people finding out about me and Rosemary being over and the revelation of me and Ava potentially being together outed on the various platforms which people who I know and have known get all their information from. It's hard to explain but basically somebody who spends their entire existence browsing social media stumbling upon my failed relationship and having a view on it or any kind of feelings towards it, makes me angry. Of course, I'm more immune to this possibility than most. Rosemary and I never entered in to the 'Date night with this one' or 'Paris with this one', posted with the customary awkward photo, behaviour. When did the 'with this one' thing even begin? Who decided that was a good idea? Couples constantly posting up everything they do together. When will it end? 'Waiting for social services to come over with this one', with a selfie attached which shows their kids in the background bruised and battered. 'Sitting in marriage counselling with this one', with a big smiling photo of the couple hugging. Fuck these kinds of people; they're bloody annoying. And when it all goes tits up, they have all these photos and statuses plastered over the internet for everyone to see how fucking naïve they were. Some of course, aren't naïve. They actually know that their partner doesn't love them, but they've invested so much time into creating this façade online that they continue to do it. They ignore all the rumours of infidelity, they ignore the fact that their partner prefers going out with mates than being with them; they ignore the fact their partner is nothing like the person they want to be with, but they carry it all on anyway because the comfort of getting likes and comments on photos which show them in a loving relationship feels almost like being in a loving relationship. Although I'm not like these people, I worry that Ava might need that satisfaction at some point. She hasn't come across like she does yet, but again, it's an anxiety within me. What if she does need that comfort of seeing that I've put a photo of us up as my display photo? What if she needs me to do a Valentine's Day collage or whatever it is people do these days to show their love to everybody in meaningless ways.

Ava and I are knackered, but there's only one thing more important than sleep to us and that's food. We're hungry and we've decided to venture out tonight for a bite to eat whilst also taking in the beautiful scenery. I could bore you with descriptions, with recycled adjectives to bump up the image for you, but as you know already, if you want to know something, google it. Lorne is very beautiful. There, I said it. I couldn't help myself.

On arrival, we were greeted by the hosts' daughter. She lives in the property next door to the one we're renting, and she turned up to give us the key and the usual pleasant greeting, probably so we leave a good review. Her name's Sabrina, she's probably in her late teens and she told us to come and eat at the restaurant where she waitresses if we were looking for somewhere close by; so that's where we are sauntering into now.

We sit down and Ava catches Sabrina's eye. Sabrina, who has the biggest smile on this planet, is laughing with one of her co-workers as she notices Ava waving and drops her chat with her pal to come and see us.

"Hello guys," she says, in her strong Aussie accent.

"Hi," Ava and I say at the same time.

"Right so, I recommend the salmon."

"Are there any burgers?" I say, just begging for anything greasy to get rid of the taste of plane in my mouth.

"Yeah, sure, there's a page in the menu," Sabrina says, leaning right over me closely as she flicks through the menu onto the correct page. "Right, here."

"Cool, thanks," I say.

"I'll have the smoked salmon," Ava says.

"Great, so one salmon, and which burger?"

I just point to the biggest sounding one on the page.

"Cool, so one salmon, one Atomic Burger and can I get you any drinks?" Sabrina says, very sprightly.

"I'll just have a beer," I reply.

"Same for me please," Ava says, picking up both our menus and handing them back to Sabrina.

"I'll be as quick as I can," Sabrina says.

Ava and I nod and smile and then turn to face each other.

"You did pretty well on the plane over here considering you don't really like flying," Ava says.

"What can I say, I'm a hero who faces my fears," I reply with a grin on my face.

"Yes, so brave. I'm proud of you," Ava smiles at me.

"And I'm proud of you, for calling out those pricks on the plane," I say.

Ava begins to look a little bit sombre. She looks down and says, "Yeah, well, felt like I had to."

"You didn't have to; most people ignore that kind of stuff which means people get away with saying it out loud far too often."

She thinks for a moment and then goes to speak again, "It's just that I know a guy, who goes to my pottery club and—"

I have to interject. "Wait, what? Pottery club?" I smirk.

Ava laughs. "Yes...pottery club."

"Okay sorry, go on..." I say. Still finding the fact she goes to a pottery club amusing.

Ava breathes in heavily. "There's a guy, who goes to my...pottery club... and he is gay, and he is the nicest man ever."

"I don't go to your pottery club," I interject again. Ava jokingly hits my hand and tells me to shut up with her eyes.

"He told his family and his wife that he was gay and now he has nobody. His family left him, and he lives alone and doesn't get to see his kids and he gets death threats all the time from people who he was friends with, and I just think it's sad and ridiculous."

I put my hand on top of Ava's as I see she is passionate about this and it's making her upset.

Sabrina walks over and puts our drinks down on the table.

"Hey, I'm finishing my shift as I'm not feeling too great, but there'll be somebody over to sort you guys out in no time at all, okay?" she says.

"Thanks, I hope it's nothing too serious," Ava says as I force a smile and another nod of the head.

"No, I'll be fine," Sabrina says. Walking away and out of the restaurant.

I look at Ava. "Your friend is lucky to have you."

"Thanks," she says back.

"But I'm glad he's gay, otherwise I'll just be thinking of you and him at pottery club re-enacting the scene from *Ghost* with Demi Moore and Patrick Swayze."

Ava laughs out loud. "Ha, well, you should come along one night, and we can do that together."

"Yeah, I'm busy that night," I say, smirking and looking slightly nervous that she really wants me to do pottery club with her.

Ava smiles at me and we take another sip of our drinks.

After dinner, Ava and I take a slow stroll back to our apartment. We lay down on the sofa and we kiss; I think the air-con must be making us horny. We've yet to have sex, but, I bloody love kissing her. I love how she kisses me, like she enjoys doing it. I don't think there's anything much better than kissing somebody who wants to kiss you as much as you want to kiss them. We've all been in a position where we've been drunk and kissed someone we didn't really want to or kissed someone during spin the bottle and got a bit of their kebab in our mouth. But sitting next to somebody, in isolation, with the waves hitting off the rocks as the only background noise, is a peaceful scenario, that I'll never know of. Because as soon as we start kissing, we are disturbed by the volume on what can only be described as an 'Ibiza style' sound system which starts blaring next door. Ironically, it is playing the same song that was playing during mine and Ava's first kiss, but this time, the walls are pulsating and not my beating heart (cringe).

When me and Ava first kissed, it was many weeks into my physio and I had finally decided to stop milking the pain and agreed to go and play some pool with her at a local bar. I wasn't drinking, which meant for the first time in my life, I had a first kiss, sober. Not sure if that's sad, or just a sign of being brought up in the 'Booze Binge Britain' era. Before we started playing, we had a few bets. It started off just funny things like 'loser has to pay for the cinema'. To her credit, Ava stuck to this particular bet. She paid for us to go to an outdoor cinema on top of a roof where we watched *The Godfather 2*. I had of course already seen it, but Ava hadn't. She came out of it saying it was a great film, only to then say, "I'll need to see the first one now." She's beautiful inside and out, but I'm sure she tries to wind me up by doing shit like that. Anyway, eventually we set up our last game of pool; as she put the white ball down to take the break, Ava said, "If I win, you have to kiss me, deal?"

I was kind of taken aback, I wasn't sure if that was something I wanted to do. I still had all sorts of issues and feelings going on and kissing somebody else other than Rosemary had become scary for some reason. "You're not going win, so it doesn't matter," I said as I watched Ava smash the balls with the white cue ball.

During the game, Ava ran over to the jukebox and was excited to see they had some tracks belonging to 'Dave Matthews Band' (her favourite band if you remember) and she decided to pick one and proceeded to dance around the table, cue in hand, potting balls, whilst singing out the words loudly for the rest of the bar to hear. She smiled and she looked really happy. It was in this moment that I remembered why I looked at her in the first place. I didn't know at Gerry's funeral that I would start to have feelings for her, but, watching her again, just being herself, fuck. I knew it there that I wanted to kiss her. But we didn't kiss to Dave Matthews Band. As the game came down to its close conclusion, it was a black ball game and it was my shot. Somebody in the bar had just put on Tiesto - Adagio for Strings. The clubby beat had ended, and it hit that slow-moving part; you know the bit that they played in the movie *Platoon*? (Shout out Samuel Barber). I hit the cue ball, it bounced off the black and I watched the black ball go flying into the pocket. "Oh," Ava said, in a disappointed tone. I laughed, a genuine laugh. As I did, I noticed the white ball come spinning back towards me and stop just short of going in the pocket. Ava looked at me and stuck out her bottom lip. I grinned, kneed the table gently, and watched the white ball fall into the pocket. Ava won. She had a massive smile on her face and walked around the table and gave me a huge hug. She looked at me and said, "You're an idiot."

Then, kissed me. I kissed her back.

So here we are, on our apparent relaxing trip to Australia, trying to kiss some more, whilst next door plays the Tiesto version of Adagio for Strings at full volume, at midnight. Ava is getting irritated. I'm not; I'm continuing the stress ban by pretending I can't hear the music or see the walls vibrating around us. Ava gets up off the sofa, walks out of the front door and starts storming towards Sabrina's place. I follow her.

"Just so you know, if there's a cat fight and you're getting your hair pulled, I can't help," I shout after Ava, trying to keep up with the mad woman as she leaves our apartment in a rage. "Hello, Ava. I'm supposed to be relaxing and recovering not refereeing," I shout out again, but the girl has bolted.

I finally get to Sabrina's front door; Ava is waiting for me. We knock on the door but there's no answer so we both look through the windows to see that there's some kind of house party in full swing in the living room. We walk around the back of the property and can hear people in the back garden. I stand up on a rock to help see over the fence and to my surprise, I see three girls lying back in a swimming pool with their tits out. Obviously, my eyebrows raise slightly and then I look away when I notice that Ava has pulled herself up to peer over the fence and has also noticed the tits. She looks at me. She knows I've seen the tits and I'm not mentioning the tits, so she's now suspicious that I haven't mentioned the tits and she's thinking I liked seeing the tits and it's just getting stressful. I should have brought my notepad. I don't know where to look.

"They've got their tits out in the garden," Ava says sternly.

"Have they?" I shrug. Scrunching my face up like I don't know what she's on about.

"Yes, there's very pretty girls over the other side of this fence and they've got their tits out," Ava says, not even bloody blinking.

"Didn't see them," I say, fidgeting about trying to find somewhere else to look.

"Do you want to jump over and see the tits Johnny?" Ava says, raising her own eyebrows.

I don't know what the right answer is. If I say no, she might think I can't go over and be around tits because I'll like the tits;

if I say yes, it means I want to see the tits. It's tough being a man.

"No," I squirm, unsure of what she wants me to say.

"Pity, I do," Ava says, turning around quickly and pulling herself up and over the fence.

I'm now standing in the middle of the street on my own. I wait a minute, calling out for Ava with no response. I look about, twiddling my thumbs, remembering to act before anxiety hits. With that thought, I run towards the fence, jump up onto the rock and then pull myself over the fence and into the garden. I land with a bit of a thud. Ava is nowhere to be seen. There are a few young people looking at me as I dust myself down though and as I pick myself up and wander through the crowds of people looking for Ava, somebody hands me a drink.

"Hello mate," a male voice says, whilst putting his arm around me. The bloke is clearly drunk but he's friendly enough and I decide to drink from the beer he's given me, hoping it's not laced with Rohypnol. I'm also slightly distracted by the fact he looks like a cross between Buzz from *Home Alone* and Biff from *Back to the Future*.

"What's going on mate? My name's Clive."

"I'm Johnny," I say, trying not to pass out due to his stinking alcohol breath. Is this the breath we all have when we're drunk but can't smell it because we're drunk? If so, I'm giving up alcohol for life. I'm nearly gagging.

"Gawssh, there's so many women here," Clive says, nearly at the point of orgasming.

"Yeah there is," I say, looking around.

"There's some in the pool over there, and they've got their tits out, have you seen 'em?" Clive mutters with a gleeful look on his face.

"No, I've not seen them," I say, expressionless.

With that, Clive takes me by the arm and decides to escort me over to the pool area. He sits down on a sun lounger.

"Sit down mate. Come on, we can look from here," Clive says, getting overly excited now.

He bangs his glass of beer against mine and sighs.

"I love tits," he says in his strong Aussie accent. Are all the accents this strong?

I nod and take a sip of my beer. I also quickly look over my shoulder to see if I can see Ava coming to save me from this hellish situation.

"How about you?" Clive inquires.

"How about me what?" I say.

"Tits," Clive says.

"Oh, yeah, they're alright I suppose."

"Just alright!?" Clive bellows. "Nah, they're fucking heavenly."

"Are they?" I ask.

"Yeah, they're like the wonders of the world or things that are so incredible that you just can't explain them," Clive says passionately.

There's an awkward silence as he continues to stare at the tits and I continue to check behind me for Ava.

Clive continues his ardent explanation of why tits are so amazing. "Yeah, they're like waterfalls or rainbows or other shit that is just unexplainable."

"I'm pretty sure people can explain waterfalls and rainbows to be honest," I say.

"Fine," Clive says. "They're like Car Boners."

"What?" I ask.

"You know when you're in the car and for no reason you just get a boner? I don't know what you call them in the UK but here we call them 'Car Boners'. Because you know, you're in a car—"

"And you get a boner," I interrupt. "Yeah, I get it."

And he's got me with that one. I can't explain 'Car Boners'.

After some other odd chats with Clive about 'why people pose for photos with their dying grandparents in their hospital bed' and 'the fact that plastic straws make up just 2000 tons of 9 millions tons of plastic which enter the water each year but certain food chains ban them to appease the simple-minded people who see a photo of a tortoise with a straw up its nose so it looks like the company are doing something for the environment when they're actually just averting your attention away from the fact they continue to avoid paying tax', I got up, and went to look for Ava.

It's weird being at a party full of young people enjoying life and seemingly not having a care in the world. The last party I remember being at was with Rosemary when we went to her cousin's engagement party some years ago. We had stopped going on nights out by this point, but we unfortunately bumped into her cousin Karen at the train station whilst on the way to visit Rosemary's mum and dad. I don't think we were going to be invited initially but it was one of those situations where Karen felt like she had to invite us, and we felt like we had to accept.

The party was in a local football team's club house and the hall was kitted out with loads of photos of Karen and her new fiancé Benjamin. I didn't know him, but five minutes in his presence, I knew he was the kind of 'lad' who loved beer with a bit of lemonade in it, phoning up Babestation and turned up to his local night club if a *Love Island* contestant was doing a PR guest appearance. Him and his friends were clones of each other. They had the same slicked back hairstyle, said 'do you know what I mean' after every sentence and all dressed like they were extras in *TOWIE*. They were from Ruislip, or some other middle-class suburb of London, but spoke like they were the love children of Dick Van Dyke and Danny Dyer. I was introduced to the circle of men and introduced myself back, hoping that would be the end of our communication, but I had to stay in the fucking circle because Rosemary wandered off with her cousin. The next 45 minutes consisted of me trying to make my pint of beer last whilst listening to these blokes bang on about football. At the end of the day, I love football as much as the next person, but I can also acknowledge that it's just 22 blokes kicking around a leather sphere on some grass whilst getting abused by thousands of 'fans' who would throw their loved ones in front of a train just to be the person who they're calling a 'cunt'. It's importance in the grand scheme of life are nil and quite frankly, I was bored of listening to these clowns blabber on about the pros and cons of VAR. I soon realised that I was in one of those situations where everybody is speaking apart from me. You soon start to count the times that everybody speaks to make sure there's somebody else not speaking to make you feel better, but everybody is speaking, and I know that they're thinking that I'm not speaking and it's just fucking awkward. Usually when I see somebody in the position I was in then, I purposely ask them a question to get them in on the conversation; unfortunately for me, these lot liked the sound of their own voices and their dim-witted pointless conversation was just becoming a buzzing sound in my head. I needed to find the right way to break into the conversation without appearing to interrupt rudely. As the 'banter' was edging up a notch into vulgarity, I tried to change the mood slightly. The boys were 'bantering' about the alleged David Beckham affair with his PA Rebecca Loos and talking about how they would have done the same thing. I wasn't really interested in hearing a bunch of gimpy blokes talk about what they'd do in bed with a woman in a hypothetical situation. The boys gurned and laughed out loud at their sex talk but as the over-the-top howling came to a quiet halt, I took my chance and piped up with what I thought was a very amusing fact.

153

"Did you know David Beckham was born in a hospital called Whipps Cross?"

"What?" Benjamin said, as the other men's faces succumbed to a confused look.

"Yeah, Whipps Cross Hospital, in Leytonstone, East London, you know?" I said.

"Nah not really," Benjamin said.

"Oh," I said, whilst looking at the other men to see if they knew what I was talking about. They didn't. "Well yeah, he was born there," I said, trying to resuscitate the story.

"And…" one of Benjamin's friends muttered.

I couldn't fucking take it anymore. I snapped.

"The hospital is called Whipps Cross mate. David Beckham is famous for whipping in crosses; it's not fucking hard, is it? I haven't drawn you a maths problem and asked you to solve it and write me out the bloody answer in Chinese."

I went on a bit of a further rant, which resulted in a kind of brawl like debacle and we were asked to leave.

I thought Rosemary was going to be angry at me, but she wasn't. She was the one who told me the David Beckham/Whipps Cross story years before. "What a bunch of wankers," she said on hearing the news that they didn't find that piece of information amusing. It was the first time in a long while we laughed together, went for a drink and got home and had sex. Nine months later, Samuel was born.

As I walk into the house of the party I'm currently at, the air con hits me and I feel my penis shrivel up and I think it's gone to hide in my stomach. Ava is nowhere to be seen downstairs, so I venture upstairs hoping that I'll be able to find her and escape because this party is starting to make me feel old.

After accidentally walking into a room where two people were fumbling underneath the covers, I walk out and hear some whimpering coming from down the hallway. The Sherlock in me follows the said whimpering and I end up by a door near the toilet. I open it to find Ava sitting on a bed, holding Sabrina. Not in the kind of lesbian kinky fantasy way. Sabrina is crying and Ava is looking after her. Ava looks up at me and ushers me out with one hand as she strokes Sabrina's hair with the other. I close the door softly, and head back to our gaff.

Whilst I wait for Ava to return, I crack open a beer in our apartment and sit down on the couch to watch some Australia television. It's 10% TV shows, 90% adverts for anybody who's interested in the show to advert ratio. Alone, and slightly tipsy, I get the overwhelming feeling to read the letter that Rosemary left

155

me at the hospital after my accident. I've put it off for so long and I'm not entirely sure why. I have a bunch of feelings that are hard to explain, and unexplainable feelings are the worst kind of feelings of all possible feelings. I grab the letter and sit on the sofa.

Johnny

I know when you wake up and find out that things have changed, you're going to want answers. I don't currently feel like you deserve anything from me but I'm trying to find the decency in my heart to help you. I'm going to write this letter to the man whose body I lay over in the street and not the man who I now know you really are. A man who betrayed me.

I've read all the messages between you and Ava. I'm sorry if you feel like this was wrong, but once I read one, I had to read them all. The lump in my throat and sickness in my stomach after reading your conversations will stay with me for a long time. It's weird, because I feel like if they were sexual in nature, I could have forgiven you, but they were much worse than that. They were more intimate than flirting or sex or any of that other stuff you would expect a cheating man to be saying.

156

You told her about your feelings, and she told you about hers. Private, personal things that a human being would only tell somebody who they trusted. Whether you knew it or not, by speaking on this level, you were giving Ava your heart over time and you were accepting her heart in return. You were giving her something that belonged to me, and you were throwing my heart away so you could accept hers. That's what hurts the most.

I don't even hate Ava. We went for coffee at the hospital when she first came to see you and we spoke a lot. She was brave and she faced me and there were a lot of tears. She told me she didn't mean to fall in love with you, but she did. She knew that what she was doing wasn't okay, but you became a person she relied on.

She did say something that hurt me though. She said that when she met you at the wedding, you seemed like someone who was so full of life but wasn't allowed to show it. She saw me and felt like I was someone who was holding you back from being yourself. It wasn't until she found out about our past that she realised why I was like I was, and she apologised for her first impression. She made many apologies over the weeks, but she did not apologise for loving you.

She was right though. I have held you back. My inability to move forward from Lucy's death is the reason why you haven't been able to. I've watched you try your hardest to make life work and to make us happy again, but my weakness has exhausted your strength. I did blame you for what happened with Lucy. I blamed you because you blamed yourself and I needed somebody to blame, so blaming you was the easiest thing to do. You were there and you took the brunt of my anger. Whilst I moved on with others around me, your face reminded me of our daughter's face and the pain of her death came back every time. I don't want you to think I didn't try to move on because I did, but maybe I left it too late. When we started to get back on track (and at times I felt like we did), something would remind me of everything bad that had happened, and it would just bring me and us back to square one.

I love you, you stupid man. I have done since the night we met, and I will always love you for everything we've shared together in our lifetime.

You'll always be a part of my life because Samuel will always be a part of yours.

I don't know where you go from here with your life, but I honestly hope it's towards happiness.

Rosemary

I bite my top lip with my bottom teeth. The tears want to come but they don't, almost like they've had enough of falling. Instead, my jaw does that thing where it aches because the tears want to come out. I know that makes no sense, unless you're one of those people whose jaw hurts when they're trying not to cry. It's fucking horrible to come to the realisation that you won't be with the person you've spent so much of your life loving. That there will end up being someone else who knows them best and the even worse fear that nobody will ever know or love you better. As I process the fear, Ava walks through the front door.

CHAPTER 8

It turned out that Sabrina was an alcoholic. Her mother had sent her to their holiday home to recover in peace, away from the bright lights and distractions of her city life in Sydney and a boyfriend that her mum didn't approve of. The tactic didn't work as nobody kept an eye on her, so she just organised nightly parties and drank herself stupid whilst indulging in rampant unsafe sex with numerous men, and women. That's what Ava told me anyway. Ava's taken Sabrina under her wing and for the past few weeks, she's become somewhat of a guardian. "She's young and naïve and we need to help her get back on the straight and narrow," Ava said to me whilst we got ready for bed the night of that big party and the tears, and the tits.

I had a browse of myself in the bedroom mirror as I got into bed that night. I saw myself laugh whilst looking at my reflection, knowing full well that I would describe myself as a Leonardo Di Caprio lookalike before I ever saw myself as a good poster boy for the 'straight and narrow' lifestyle. If I die, it's the words of Marlon Brando as Terry Malloy in *On the Waterfront* that I want on my gravestone. "You don't understand! I coulda had class. I coulda been a contender. I could've been somebody. Instead of a bum, which is what I am - let's face it."

I said that to Ava recently and she replied, "Stop being a self-pitying dickhead and get a grip."

I shrugged and stuck my tongue out at her like a six-year-old child. She laughed, but I meant it.

Every morning of our trip since that party, Sabrina comes over for breakfast and a chat. She's here now, looking for cereal. Ava makes sure she hasn't Phil Mitchell'd herself to death and I engage in as little discussion as possible. The problem is, Ava's main tactic for helping Sabrina is trying to show empathy and thus revealing intimate private information in an attempt to relate. This is a bad thing for me because now Sabrina knows things about my life which she brings up at inappropriate times. At first, I thought she was trying to 'Lolita' me into bed but then I remembered I'm not Jeremy Irons and Sabrina was just one of those people who got enjoyment out of winding people up. That, luckily, we have in common. I like annoying idiots and she likes annoying idiots. She thinks I'm an idiot and I knew pretty early on she was an idiot.

"Why didn't you marry your ex-girlfriend?" Sabrina says, stopping me in my tracks, mid bite of an apple. (I eat apples now too; Ava feeds me healthy food.)

"What has that got to do with anything?" I say.

Sabrina shrugs her shoulders and starts pouring an annoying amount of cornflakes into her bowl.

"That's going to overflow when you put the milk in," I say.

"Oh well," Sabrina says, as she continues to pour milk.

It overflows.

I get up to get a cloth to wipe down the milky table as Sabrina begins to get started again on her line of questioning.

"So, your ex," she begins.

"I don't really want to talk about this to be honest Sabrina; how about we talk about how you're doing?"

"I'm fine. Why didn't you marry your ex?"

"I wasn't, well I'm not, a believer in marriage."

"Why not?"

"Why so? I think that's more of an important question," I say, throwing the milky cloth into the washing machine.

"Because it's a thing people do; everybody does it," Sabrina says, taking a mouthful of cornflakes after finishing her sentence.

"Don't you think everybody does it, because everybody does it?" I ask her back.

Sabrina shrugs at my answer.

"If nearly everybody didn't get married, most people wouldn't get married," I say. "The issue my generation and your generation has is that we get to see in detail all of these people doing all of these things and we think that's the way things need to be done in order to be good or normal and at the end of the day, people find comfort in normality."

"So, you're a rogue to normality then?"

"No. I just think marriage isn't necessary for me. I didn't love Rosemary less or more because marriage wasn't part of our lives."

"Did she feel like you loved her less though because you didn't want to get married?" Sabrina asks. Then proceeds to drink the leftover milk from her cereal, using both hands to tip the bowl towards her mouth.

"Rosemary didn't want to get married," I tell Sabrina.

Sabrina puts the bowl down.

"How do you know? You never asked," she says. "I bet you subtly put your views about marriage into conversations early on in the relationship and she knew you didn't want to get married so never felt to mention it again. She loved you enough to know marriage wasn't something you wanted to do, but maybe you didn't love her enough to realise marriage was something she did want to do?"

"I loved her enough," I say, now getting bored and irritated by her brashness.

"Enough to cheat?" she barks back with a smirk.

"I never cheated."

"As good as," Sabrina replies.

"Not really, but listen, you're naïve; you're young and you have this idea in your head about what's right and wrong and there's no in-between with people like you," I respond, knowing full well I'm getting irate, but trying to stay sarcastically calm.

"You cheated, and you know you did," Sabrina says back, standing up, picking up her dish and dropping it into the sink. She goes and sits back down at the table.

"Did you put vodka in those cornflakes?" I ask her.

"Oh, low blow," Sabrina says, but doesn't show any signs of being fazed by my remark.

"Just asking," I fake smile. "I might have a drink, do you mind?"

"Drinking before midday, some may say you have an issue Johnny," Sabrina says.

I take two shot glasses out of the cupboard and fill them both up with whiskey. I sit down at the table opposite Sabrina and put them down.

"People like you Sabrina, have this romantic version of life that doesn't exist. It's bullshit and you can't see it's bullshit because you're too busy trying to recreate it. You're trying to be this broken, tortured soul who's an addict and will probably die young. Your heroes are probably other broken, tortured souls, who have died young and you almost certainly think to yourself in your deluded state that you're somewhat like them. Let me tell you something, there's nothing romantic about dying young. It's bullshit. Growing and living is fucking romantic. It's a damn privilege to grow old. You're taking that fact for granted."

"You don't know anything," Sabrina says.

"I do. You think I'm a dick, because I cheated, because I've come here, and it looks like I've run away from my problems. Maybe that's true. But people make mistakes, and good people

165

fuck up. They fuck up even when they know they're fucking up. You're thinking that you quite like Ava and the 'once a cheat, always a cheat' logic means I'm going to hurt her."

"Not really, I think Ava's quite vanilla actually," Sabrina chimes in.

"Well, you can think whatever you like, but she's the only one who gives a shit about you. I don't. I'd happily sit here and get drunk with you right now," I say, pushing the shot glass nearer to her.

Sabrina looks down at the drink.

"You're not an alcoholic; you're just being a dick," I declare. "Alcoholism is a disease which tears people apart. I've watched you over these last few weeks and you haven't even thought about having a drink because you've been too busy enjoying being around us. It's the attention you crave, not the booze."

I see Sabrina's eyes well up with tears.

"Now you might have me down to a tee, but you don't know shit about yourself and when it comes down to it, judging me and having a view about my behaviour isn't going to help you with your life."

"I fucking hate you," Sabrina says as she wipes a tear from her face.

166

"Join the club."

I stand up, pick up the shot glasses from the table and pour the whiskey down the sink. Whilst my back is turned, Sabrina speaks.

"You know, Ava was right about you. You are like that bloke, in that film."

"What film?" I turn around and say.

"Before she left mine the other night, she saw that a film called *A Bout de Souffle* was on television and she told me to watch it. It was in French with subtitles."

I pass Sabrina a tissue to wipe away the remainder of her tears.

"She said you reminded her of the main character. His name was Michael."

"How so?" I ask.

"I think it must have been the line where Michael says, 'I always get interested in girls who aren't right for me'."

"Ava's right for me," I respond quickly.

"Is she?" Sabrina asks.

"Do you ever learn from your mistakes?" I ask Sabrina.

"What? You've just made a young girl cry and you can't answer a question," Sabrina says, with her strong Aussie accent in tow.

"You're not young; in a few years' time, you'll be the same age I was when my daughter died."

Sabrina nods, "Sorry."

"I admire you for trying to come back for Round 2 of interrogating questions with me, but I promise you, there's nothing you can ask me that I haven't asked myself," I say, calmly and nicely.

"Between grief and nothing, I will take grief. Which would you choose?" Sabrina says softly.

"What?" I ask, confused.

"It's from the French film. They discuss that question and I'm asking you the same thing."

I think about the question for a moment before I respond.

"I wouldn't wish grief on anybody, not the grief I've felt and seen, but with life, comes death, and unfortunately, grief follows. It has for me; it will for you."

Sabrina looks sombre. I feel a bit of sadness in my gut for her.

"All right, I'll count to eight, and if you haven't smiled, I'll strangle you," I say loudly.

Sabrina looks up and smiles straight away.

"So, you have seen the film?" she says.

"I'm going out with Ava; of course I've seen the bloody film," I smile, and Sabrina and I laugh together. I slightly shy away for a moment to contemplate what I've just said in regards to mine and Ava's relationship status. What actually are we?

Anyway, talking of laughing. Ava has begun to write her book. During one of our first nights together, she was telling me that she wants it to be a serious drama, with some comedy and eventually, in the end, everybody's happy. I told her to give up on her dream of writing and there began one of our first fights. I of course was joking, kind of. I support her dream of writing, but at the same time, no good book ever ended with the word 'laughing'. After she gently kicked me in the balls and got me in a headlock, she said, "I'm being serious; I just want it to end with everybody laughing."

"Impossible," I said to her.

"We'll see," she said.

Lying in bed with Ava now, watching her as she sleeps, it feels

169

peaceful and safe. I've mentioned to people before that when you live in London and you leave your house everyday with the anxiety that you might get blown up or stabbed, it's easy to forget this isn't really a normal way to live, it's a way we've allowed ourselves to live. The peacefulness and calmness of Lorne has opened my eyes to how different life can be if you allow yourself to break free from the chains in which you were born in. London is almost an identity to me, and it's not really one which I have much love for anymore. The problem is, I've built my life on those foundations and it'll be tough to dig them up and get everything I need and want to move somewhere else.

I've just woken up from a mad lucid dream about a terrorist attack in London. I managed to hide in a car situated in a car park, but the driver got in and drove away. During the panic-filled carnage, I saw England footballer Danny Rose reverse his car into the actor David Tennant's car. Danny was apologetic but said he needed to get to the airport because he was going to miss the 2018 World Cup. David then got a piece of paper and a pen out of his pocket and tried to do some maths to work out why football mattered. I woke up with the sweats.

I'm not sure why I'm having these thoughts and dreams but maybe it's to do with having to go back home soon and I'm subconsciously nervous. Maybe I'm dreaming about the 2018 World Cup because that was a glimpse into how good and happy our country can be, whereas the years before and the years after are a reminder of how bad it is. Maybe David Tennant was there because I need to see a doctor when I get home to check if it's okay for me to go back to work. Who knows, but I'm here now, in the last few days of our trip, filling out forms online trying to find a job. Back to being irritated by being asked about 'My Religion', 'My Race', 'My Gender' and then being told it's not what they judge applications on. How about you don't ask then? If you don't know, you can't discriminate!

I read an article in an Australia magazine yesterday about a man who got sacked from his job for being racist towards an Aboriginal Australian co-worker. It turned out he didn't actually say anything racist; he just disagreed with his co-worker's definition of 'racism'. It turned out that groups can now create their own definition and if they say that's the definition, you can't disagree or you're Hitler. There was a similar issue some years back now where a Muslim organisation drafted up a definition of 'Islamophobia' which the UK Government rejected on the grounds that the definition was too broad and didn't allow for debate or criticism. Of course, religion, is just an idea that should be allowed to be freely mocked for how ridiculous it is. Then there's things that cannot be changed like the colour of your skin. There are also groups who like to spruce up the definition of 'racism' to suit their agenda or exclude certain

171

people from discussion on topics whom they believe can't have a good input because it doesn't affect them. I was having some pre-drinks at mine when I was in my late teens when one of my mates got robbed on the bus in Camden. He was robbed by five South Asian looking boys who were all calling him 'white boy' and 'British boy' as they did it - which made little sense because according to my mate they all had British accents with a slight twang of faux Jamaican. He never went to the police; he just accepted it like many people do in London these days, as if it's part of the culture to be robbed on British transport, or, if you're a female lesbian couple who don't want to kiss for the enjoyment of men, you can expect to be beaten up (google it). What shocked me the most is when he told his girlfriend, who in my opinion was one of those self-loathing hippy do-gooders, she was sad, but tried to correct him when he told her it was a racist attack. "It wasn't racist because you're white and racism is the systemic oppression of minorities caused by white people."

She was white of course, middle class, and her name was Daisy; and I've not met anyone with the name Daisy who wasn't a bit of a cunt to be honest. She went on some hippy do-gooder rant about 'white people having power'. Well my friend didn't have the power that day and as far as I'm concerned, anybody can be racist and the 'shut up you're white; you can't have a view unless it's the same view as mine' rhetoric can fuck off. We will not beat racism with racism. We will not beat racism by marginalising people with different lived experiences. And we definitely won't beat racism by following trends just to fit into societies expectations of what's good and proper.

This new social justice warrior trend and unwitty belittling catchphrases like 'white fragility' are unhelpful. They are divisive. People who partake in it will obviously shout 'irony' and tell me I'm 'proving their point', which is why the whole belief system is fucking moronic. It would be like me saying 'there's a giant talking golden bear who comes into my house sometimes and eats all my dinner, and if anybody says it's not true then they're phobic towards talking bear enthusiasts'. Somebody might say 'well where's the evidence' and I'll say, 'my dinners gone' and they'll say, 'well there's obviously numerous other potential reasons why it's gone' and I'd say, 'exactly'. Their belief system begins as fact and not just a created concept, and the norm now is to call anybody who wants to question their perceived facts, a 'bad person'. And that doubters or non-believers should die. Basically.

There are other futile insults which are also directed at black people who don't follow the narrative that people with their skin colour are expected to follow. 'Uncle Tom', 'Race traitor', amongst others. It's not like me to defend the Tories but the people on the end of these insults are usually black conservatives who don't believe they are oppressed, don't believe their country is racist and hate identity politics. I don't know whether they're right or wrong, but I know that they should be entitled to their view without being bullied into silence. Silence isn't going to fix the problem. Intelligent dialogue will.

Point is when you start using terms like 'white fragility' as if it's a scientific fact instead of a fallacy coined due to idiotic pseudoscience then you become more like Hitler than those who you call Hitler. Judging demographics has led to some of the most horrendous events in history after all. The 'progressive left' don't really care about being progressive though. They prefer to be 'woke', which apparently means battling racism with racism. It means judging all white people (white men in particular) yet condemning white people who judge other races, religions or cultures. The only real social justice is to mock the contradictions of this hypocritical mindless rhetoric. The followers of Robin DiAngelo (who coined the term 'white fragility') and her ideology in Britain have most likely already been influenced by the mass influx of American media/social issues in our news feeds and because they yearn for answers to how they feel about their own lives and experiences, they are susceptible to passionate scribblings oiled up in Marxism. Hey, even I once upon a time felt like Robin Hood when I was stealing sweets after school from the newsagent's. Until I realised, I was just stealing off a man who was like me but got a job. There is classism and social mobility issues in Britain and the fact if you're born poor, you're far more likely to stay poor throughout your life and vice-versa with the rich, is an important topic and problem. It's complex, and battling it with discrimination and petulant name-calling, isn't going to get us far in making a change for the better.

I've never thought about all of this much before but bringing a child into the world changes things. As he gets older in this new age we now live in, Samuel will be part of this debate; and whilst I don't want him to be ignorant of history, I don't want him to ever feel the need to apologise for the behaviour of others and events he never partook in. It worries me that he will grow up with social media as part of his life for all of his life. I cannot imagine the level of bullying that happens in schools these days if you don't blindly follow the latest trends and aren't seen to be saying the exact same thing that is popular. This doesn't leave any room for growth if your mind is shackled by fear.

The way I've always looked at it is, if I don't experience something, I get my information from people who do. So, I don't experience homophobia, but I know it exists because I see it happen to my friends, and I hear their stories and I believe them. It's also seemingly valid to voice homophobia publicly if you back it up with 'my religion says so'. Racism, is not so publicly acceptable however. I've been with my black friends before and watched them get stopped by police and searched when there's been absolutely no reason to do so. I listen to their individual experiences. Whilst I support stop and search because fuck knows we need it and I truly believe 99.9% of police are good and use it sensibly, I still sympathise with innocent people's frustration. So anyway, if my white friend has got robbed, or feels like he was turned down for a job because of his race then I'm going to hear that and appreciate that could have been the case. No extra little bits or 'buts' added on because he's white. Racism is racism and it exists, and we all must call it out when we see it in all its forms or we're part of the problem. The world is evolving into something different and though the history books show us photos of victims who may not look like us, the next history book is just around the corner showing a new story. It's a complex issue I get it, but it's this consistent unhelpful rhetoric I've seen for a few decades where 'white' is allowed to be used openly as negative on mass without retort. It's not fragility to call bullshit on bullshit. People cry about the rise of right-wing politics but can't see that their rhetoric is a reason for the rise. You have to be able see how people may get fed up of having something they can't change about themselves in the media being used as a negative or blamed for things they never did. People are fed up of being called words like 'racist' every time they have a view on immigration or religion or culture and there will be people with ill thoughts that will tap into that irritation for votes and potentially a more harmful agenda. There is racism, we know that, but some people, and you know who you are, are watering it down with your nonsensical fuckery. Maybe it's different for me. I've grown up in multi-cultural London, where in certain places being White and British is a minority. I've always been part of a working-class community which was a tight-knit set of people from all races. I feel like I'm less ignorant for growing up here and I don't need a handbook of do's and don'ts to help me not be racist. I am sure though, there will be somebody out there who has a handbook which says that what I've just said, is very racist. Maybe I'll read it. I'm always learning.

Anyway, it was Edward Furlong as Danny Vinyard in *American History X* who said:

"So I guess this is where I tell you what I learned - my conclusion, right? Well, my conclusion is: Hate is baggage. Life's too short to be pissed off all the time. It's just not worth it. Derek says it's always good to end a paper with a quote. He says someone else has already said it best. So, if you can't top it, steal from them and go out strong. So, I picked a guy I thought you'd like. 'We are not enemies, but friends. We must not be enemies. Though passion may have strained, it must not break our bonds of affection. The mystic chords of memory will swell when again touched, as surely, they will be, by the better angels of our nature.'"

I think letting a fictional white supremacist have the final say on this topic is apt.

*****

My overthinking about things I can't really change has been a lifelong battle. Fortunately for me, Australia has allowed me to clear my mind of such thoughts and try to concentrate on the positive. I've been going for runs along the beach and been eating much healthier than I was back at home, which has led me to feeling stronger both physically and mentally. I'm looking forward more than anything, to seeing Samuel and being able to give him a big hug. Not long now.

Tonight, we're at Sabrina's because she is cooking us a meal as a thank you for not letting her drown herself in vodka. Ava and I went for a wander today and she managed to pick up a nice yellow flowery dress in one of the few shops in Lorne. I picked up an ice cream, three scoops of vanilla. After the nightmare of going dress shopping with a girl, we went to a place called Teddy's Lookout. There's a little walkway which leads to a viewing platform for a scenic view of the ocean and the mountainous area around it. Whilst up there, Ava said she loved me. I said "cute" and then finished my ice cream.

"So, how's the writing going?" Sabrina asks Ava as we all sit around the dinner table.

"Good thanks. I've got a lot done these last six weeks so it's been a productive trip."

There's a slight sense of awkwardness in the air between Ava and myself after she said "I love you" for the first time and I reacted like a man-baby. Sabrina has probably picked up on the atmosphere, but she's managed to not be her usual pot-stirring self and is currently keeping quiet.

"So, where have you got up to with the book then?" Sabrina asks, as she begins to dish out the food onto our plates.

"Well, I'm thinking about killing the main character off," Ava says.

"No! You can't do that; it'll be like when they killed off Derek in *Grey's Anatomy*. It ruined the show," Sabrina gasps.

I nod as I put a roast potato in my mouth.

"I just feel like, it's been all about him and every word or feeling is his, you know? I feel like the female characters have been pushed back into secondary characters whose views and feelings

179

are not as important as his," Ava says, whilst tucking into the food herself.

"But surely you can give the characters a voice without having to kill off the main character?" I say, trying not to speak with my mouth full.

"I want it to be true to life though. If I keep him alive, his voice will still be the loudest and most important."

The girls laugh, but the joke goes over my head as I'm enjoying the food.

"Yeah, I feel where you're coming from to be honest," Sabrina says.

"From experience?" Ava says, washing her food down with a bit of wine. (Sabrina insisted we drink, even though she isn't.)

"Yeah, my ex-boyfriend was just so noisy with his opinions and views. We were going out for about a year and his sister had a couple of kids and he used to try and make me have photos with them and put them online. Then when people asked me who they were, I just said they were my boyfriend's sister's kids, and he thought it was weird that I didn't say they were my niece and nephew."

"That's not weird," I pipe up.

"Yeah, like, I just feel as if they weren't my niece and nephew, because I guess they were already alive before I knew them, and I didn't really know his sister that well. But my ex was always on and on about how rude it was," Sabrina says, with a reminiscing look upon her face.

"Sounds like a bit of wanker to me," I say, which makes Sabrina smirk.

"Did you love him?" Ava asks.

"I thought I did, but I've come to realise that I'm not sure what love is," Sabrina responds, then looks up at me.

"You will one day; you've got a lot to offer," Ava says to Sabrina.

"Thanks. What does love mean to you Johnny?" Sabrina asks, stopping me in my tracks as I am about to put a big mouthful of food into my gob.

"Being asked to put Sudocrem on my girlfriend's bum rash and not saying no," I say without hesitation.

"Yuck," Sabrina says, grimacing.

I laugh and glimpse over at Ava, who is smirking whilst looking down at her plate.

"That's love isn't it?" I say.

"It's definitely something," Sabrina says, still looking disgusted.

"What's your plans for when we're gone then Sabrina?" Ava interrupts with.

"Party planning," Sabrina says back quickly.

Ava looks at her suspiciously.

"No, not like that. No more house parties I promise," Sabrina says whilst reaching out to squeeze Ava's hand.

"I've got a project going on where I hold these big American-style prom nights where people pay for their ticket, women come in their big gowns and men in their tuxedos and we play all the old classics and just have one big party."

"Wow," I'm taken aback a bit. "That's a good idea Sabrina." I nod at her.

"Thanks," she smiles.

CHAPTER 9

The flight home felt like it took an eternity. Ava wasn't really in a talkative mood, still obviously upset with me about not telling her I loved her back. She didn't say that, but she was withdrawn and clearly not in the mood to indulge in in-flight conversation with me. I watched some movies and I wrote in my little stress pad all the things I need to work on to stop me from losing my mind. Number one on the list was to spend more time with Samuel and focus on him; that way I won't be stressed about how he views me. I don't want to be seen as an absent father who doesn't care, and I know that once that impression is instilled into someone, it's hard for it to leave, whether it's warranted or not. So, when I eventually got home, I dropped my bags down, had a shower, got changed and headed out the door to see my boy.

I skyped Samuel a few times whilst in Australia, so I knew Rosemary and he were still living with her mum. Cheryl, as I've mentioned before, could be quite vindictive if she wanted to be, but we got on well. What I liked about her is that whilst she adored Rosemary, she wouldn't just blindly take her side or show complete contempt for anyone who upset her. In the weeks after my accident, she called me many times to see if I was okay, and never once mentioned anything to do with Ava. She just kept saying, "Get back up on your feet because you're not going to reach happiness without doing a little walking."

She loved making up a wise quote.

I reached Cheryl's house where I knocked on the door, looking forward to seeing Samuel's face. For some reason, I was nervous, questioning whether all fathers who are separated from the mother of their child feel the same when they turn up to see their kid. Like this was a test. That I had to make this time with Samuel count or be perfect otherwise I have failed as his dad. After a long wait, the door was answered by a confused looking Cheryl.

"Johnny?" she said, looking at me like I had been found sleeping in a pile of her washing.

"Hi Cheryl, I'm here to surprise Sam; I've just got back from Australia," I said, looking past her to see if I could see him.

"He's not here," Cheryl said, looking uneasy.

"Where is he?" I asked.

"They've gone away, on a trip for a few weeks," Cheryl said.

"Where?"

"Wales."

"Wales. Who the fuck goes on a trip to Wales?" I asked, the anger slowly overwhelming me.

"I don't know Johnny. I just know that she went to Wales with Sam…and David."

"David?"

"Yeah, David Donaldson," Cheryl said.

"DJ DAVEY D!? Why?"

"Look Johnny, Rosemary's been speaking with him and they've been out a few times and he asked her if she wanted to go on a holiday with him and she said yes."

"Holiday? Going to Wales isn't a fucking holiday."

"Calm down Johnny."

"Calm down? Rosemary's taken my son on holiday with another man and you want me to calm down," I shouted.

"Johnny, you've just swanned off to Australia and you're coming back here demanding what? That Rosemary puts her life on hold and waits around here just in case you decide you want to pop over to see Sam?" Cheryl barked at me.

"It's not like that, and you know it. Just tell me where they've gone, that's all I care about."

Didn't somebody wise once say 'don't act when you're angry'? What a load of bullshit that was. Anger is an emotion that requires action. If I'm angry and I sit down and wait for the anger to pass, I get angrier.

*****

So, after this slight barney with Cheryl, I spent the most draining hours of my life on a stuffy coach on my way to Wales. Some place in Wales that I've never heard of. Beddgelert. Google it.

I had to jump on and off coaches all day having not really slept in 24 hours. As I was on my journey and the sun set and the gloomy dark sky got darker and darker, I caught wind (excuse the pun) on the radio that a storm was approaching the area and caution was advised. I was the only person left on the coach. The driver asked me if he could drop me off 20 minutes outside of where I wanted to go, so he could get home to his kids before the storm arrived. Of course, I couldn't say no to that. Even though I wanted to.

So. Here I am. In Wales. To my profound shock, more people than just Rosemary and Davey D visit Beddgelert. As the taxi (that I had to get after the coach fiasco) drops me off, quite a few people are wandering about and it's not quite the deserted blackhole I thought it was going to be. Quite quickly, however, I realised that as the winds have grown stronger and the message of the incoming storm has spread around the village, the people who are still out are actually heading towards the local village hall for shelter. Stuck for options, and now being blown all over Wales, I decide to follow the crowd.

Entering the hall, it's like the Arrivals terminal at an airport. People are hugging each other and being welcomed in. There's also water and blankets being handed out, which I refuse as they're passed to me. Instead, I walk through the gathering of people on a quest to find Rosemary and Samuel.

"Johnny." I hear a voice behind me. One I've heard many times before.

"Hi," I say, turning to see a very confused Rosemary.

"What are you doing here?" she asks.

"I've come to see to Samuel; why else would I be here?" I say, looking around for him.

"Well, we're on holiday," Rosemary says back.

"You're in the arse-end of Wales?" Now, I look confused.

"Yes Johnny, some people go on holiday to Wales and it's been enjoyable up until this point," Rosemary barks at me.

"You can't just take my son—," I try to say more before being interrupted.

"He's my son. I can take him where I want, when I want. And don't follow me here, playing the Father's for Justice card when you've pissed off to Australia for months."

"You know I had to get away," I said.

"Samuel's fine Johnny. You don't need to be here; go home."

I shake my head in frustration, giving Rosemary one last glance as I walk away. Just as I bustle myself through the packed hall the doors slam shut.

"Can I have everybody's attention please?"

'For fuck sake', I think to myself. Davey D has hopped up onto a table to look down on everyone and make an announcement. Rosemary walks through a few people and stands next to me.

"What is he, the captain of this operation?" I ask her, but not taking my eyes off the burly idiot on the table, hoping with every fibre of my being that the legs will give way.

"His parents are from here, and they're pretty well known in the community."

188

"Oh well done; pretty well known by who? The eight people who live here?"

"Apparently the 2011 census had it at about 455," Rosemary says, leaning in to whisper the facts to me.

"Oh, they all must be in here then," I say sarcastically.

"Well, you're here, and you don't live in Beddgelert," Rosemary says back.

"Good," I lean back into Rosemary and whisper somewhat aggressively.

Davey D starts his announcement.

"We've just had confirmation from the authorities that no trains, planes or automobiles will be travelling in or out of the village for the foreseeable future. Whoever is in the village hall now, stays in the village hall until the storm has passed, so please get as comfortable as you can."

I sigh loudly. Irritated further by Davey D's enthusiasm for a shit situation and the fact he referenced one of my favourite films. John Candy will be rolling in his grave. Rosemary looks at me and tries to hand me a blanket. I refuse it.

When I was a kid, I went on typical working-class holidays. Not abroad, but to caravan sites. I remember my mum and dad would

189

save all year and collect vouchers in newspapers just so they could take me and my sister to Clacton or Great Yarmouth. At the time, you are kind of jealous of your friends because they come back after summer holidays talking about all these exotic places that they have been to and you have to try and big up Bognor Regis. I mean, it can be fun, but it's not Bali is it?

I also went on a week-long primary school trip; does that count as a holiday? I can't remember exactly where it was but it was a kind of summer camp place where you did things like rock climbing and toasting marshmallows over a campfire. I remember it well because I had to share a bunk bed with a kid called Timothy. Timothy was a nice boy but he was spectacularly odd. He used to come into school every day and let people know all the bad news that was happening in the world. He compiled lists of people who had died and would spend the day asking people if they knew 'so and so' had passed away. Sometimes, it was a famous celebrity and sometimes, it was just a random bloke who fell off his ladder that made it into page 19 of the local gazette. The teachers used to nod and smile, saying things like 'that's nice Timothy', but I also overheard them referring to him as 'The Tim Reaper', so even they thought he was a bit of an oddball.

Timothy, on one night, pissed the bed. He was on the top bunk, and I woke up dazed and confused, thinking the roof was leaking. It wasn't. Another person who either smelt or heard the dripping was a girl called Zoputan. She came to our school a bit later than everybody else as her family came over from Nigeria. She is part-Nigerian and her father is from Ghana I think. When Zoputan came to England, she couldn't speak one bit of English, but by the time she left primary school, she could speak it better than anybody, even all the English kids. I remember she was super smart, proper grown-up for her age and very kind. Which was shown to me on the night when Timothy pissed himself. Hearing all the commotion, she came over, rubbed her eyes, saw Tim had pissed the bed and said, "Don't worry; it happens." She then proceeded to take Timothy's covers off his bed and swap them with her covers. A few hours later when everybody woke up, there was a raucous going on in the bedroom where other students were taking the mick out of Zoputan, saying she wet herself in the night. The teachers made it worse, by coming over to her and saying things like 'Oh have you had an accident darling?'- drawing even more attention to an already embarrassed kid. Those teachers didn't have a brain cell to rub together. As the taunting went on, Timothy watched on, but not being able to take the injustice of what was happening, climbed down off the top bunk and shouted at the top of his lungs, "It wasn't her; it was me!"

Everybody gathered around, looking confused. I stood up too, so I could have a good view of the drama. "It was me who pee'd myself," Timothy said again. I think he was expecting some kind of 'I am Spartacus' moment where everybody said it was them and nobody had to live with the shame of what happened. That romantic idea was washed away forever however, when I piped up with, "Yeah, it's true. Tim pissed the bed and Zoputan swapped sheets."

Everybody then went back to laughing at Timothy and sung football chants along the lines of, 'He knows when someone's dead, and he wets the bed'. Timothy had to put up with those songs until the day we left primary school. He got picked on a bit after that but Zoputan was always there to save him. Which isn't that surprising when you learn what her name means. Google it.

I know some people might be hoping that Tim and Zoputan are out there now, together. Soulmates. They're not. Tim became an undertaker. I think he did have crush on Zoputan but I learnt years later that it was actually me, who was her favourite. I was doing jury service at this trial for a crime that I still cannot talk about, whilst Zoputan was the lawyer for a bloke who killed his whole family in a trial taking place next door. I overheard a few people talking about it in the waiting area, which, if you've done jury service, you'll know you're not supposed to do. Mine was something very boring that I tossed a coin for when it was decision time so there was no chance of me gossiping about it to others. Both trials finished on the same afternoon and in the corridor, Zoputan came up to me and said she remembered me from school. We had a good giggle about the past and as I went to walk away, Zoputan called out my name and I turned back around to face her.

"You were my favourite," she said.

"How come?" I ask.

"You always got my name right. Every time."

"What do you mean?"

"At school, you always said my name correctly, every time. Even now at work, I have people calling me all different things. They don't know how to pronounce Zoputan so they just guess."

"I knew how to say your name because you told me what your name was, just like my mum and dad told me what my name was, so I know how to say Johnny."

She smirked and then laughed. "You're funny," she said.

I didn't really get what was amusing but I smiled and we had a hug before we then parted ways. Forever intertwined in each other's reminiscing thanks to Tim pissing the bed.

I guess what I'm trying to say is that holidays are not always what you want them to be but the memories they leave you with can be just as good as the ones that you have from when you did go to where you wanted to go to. That being said. No good memories can be made in Wales. And I'm sticking to that belief.

*****

I feel like it's been days since I walked into this stupid hall, but I've only been here a few hours, wallowing in my own self-pity. The storm is in full swing and the wind has smashed one of the windows. People gathered around offering assistance to board it up but I just stayed where I was, sitting on the floor, up against a wall, wondering how I managed to go from the sun-filled Oz to getting blown away like Dorothy in *The Wizard of Oz*.

A little earlier, I got up to stretch my legs and had a quick look into the room where Samuel is sleeping. He looked peaceful and I had a bit of a lump in my throat when I saw how much he's grown since I went away. Now, I'm just tucked back into a corner of the hall with only my reflective thoughts for company. However, just as I close my eyes to get some sleep, Rosemary walks over with a cup of tea for me.

"Thanks," I say, as I take the cup from Rosemary's grasp.

"I know you're too stubborn to ask so I thought I'd bring you one over," she says as she sits down next to me.

I take a sip and the heat hits my cold insides straight away. I look at Rosemary and hold the hot tea to my chest.

"DJ Davey D, really?"

"Shut up Johnny," she says, rolling her eyes at me.

"What?" I sigh.

"He's a nice guy. We've been chatting and that's all you need to know," Rosemary tells me.

I shake my head. "But...it's like Holly Willoughby and her husband all over again," I say, as I take another sip of my tea.

"What does that even mean?" Rosemary says, confused and clearly irritated by my presence.

"He's punching."

"So were you," Rosemary quickly responds.

"I know."

We look at each other for a bit longer than a moment. No words, until I break the silence.

"I read your letter."

"Good," Rosemary whispers assertively.

"It made me cry," I say.

"Even better," Rosemary says with a kind smile on her face.

"Ouch."

"No, you need to cry Johnny; you need to let it out."

"Let what out?" I ask.

"Your sadness."

"I don't have sa…"

"It's not my business anymore John; you don't have to tell me one way or the other," Rosemary interrupts.

We sit in silence again and I look over to see Dave making two old ladies laugh by the table where he's also dishing out teas.

"Are you going to marry him?"

Rosemary looks over too and smiles. "It's not like that; we're just talking."

"Well, we were just talking at a bar once upon a time, now look at us. Spent most of our lives in each other's lives," I say, finishing off my tea and placing it down on the floor.

Rosemary doesn't answer. She reaches forward like she's going to take my hand, but she just picks up the cup in front of me and holds it.

"All the opportunities in the world, and people still just end up getting married; I think it's weird."

"You think everything's weird Johnny," Rosemary says.

"Not everything, just some things."

We both pause, look away from each other and around the room.

"Remember Nathaniel?" I ask Rosemary, turning to face her.

She looks back at me. "Wasn't he a mate from school who was there the night we met?"

"Yes, him. He got married the other day, and everyone from my group of mates was there apart from me and there were people there that he knew through me! I'm trying to be a bit more social so I've got back on to Facebook which I now wish I hadn't because I'm looking through these photos and just thinking 'cunts'."

"You're thinking that because you weren't invited Johnny, and why would you be?"

"No, actually. It's because they're all just their smiling and laughing and having fun and it's all bullshit."

"What's bullshit about falling in love?"

"When you force it?"

"Who said he was forcing anything?" Rosemary asks.

"I know a girl who he messaged on Tinder and he sent the same message to her friend too and they searched him on Facebook and saw we were friends and messaged me to see what he was like."

"And what did you say?"

"I said he was a dick."

"Lovely, so you stitched your mate up?"

"No"

"Yes Johnny, you did."

"No Rosemary, he stitched himself up. He was sending the same template to different girls and he got caught out."

"So maybe it was just his way of starting off a conversation."

"There's nothing romantic about throwing 500 shots and hoping one will land just because you want to be like everybody else and have someone."

"Different people have different things that they need, and some people just like to be normal and if their end goal is to be married and normal then why do you care?"

"Because it's bullshit."

"To you Johnny, not to them."

"Take Tony from work, remember him?" I ask. I'm going off on a tangent but there's time to kill and I'm getting some shit off my chest.

"The nice but creepy one?"

"Yes, the nice but creepy one. He used to try and get with the receptionist who was called Chloe, and she used to be fat and had hair like Anna Wintour but blonde, remember her?"

"Was she the one who did the pyramid scheme with the diet pills?"

"Yes, you remember!"

"Yeah, I didn't like her," Rosemary blurts out.

"Nobody did," I say.

"She added me to a Facebook group once for weight loss; I was a size 8 at the time," Rosemary said, clearly still harbouring ill feelings about it.

"Yeah, she wasn't the brightest bulb in the pack, but anyway. Tony used to try and get with her but she was bonking the bloke who delivered the mail; his name was Richard so Tony stopped trying to get with her."

"Where's this going John? I've got to go and help Dave."

"Well listen, a few months later, Tony managed to find himself a bird and he brought her to work to introduce her to everybody. She was fat, she had the Anna Wintour hair style but blonde and she waddled exactly the same as Chloe."

"So what, maybe he just has a type?"

"Or maybe there's just a type he can get so he sticks with it and there's nothing romantic about punching below your weight. Punch above it! You might not win every time but now and again you might get a knockout."

"But why do you care Johnny? This is what you're not answering."

"He's got married to her. He reached an age where that's what he wanted and he went out and got anything he could find and there's something sad about that. If marriage never existed and we brought it up as an idea now, people would put us in a home for being weirdos, but because it's been around for centuries and has been passed down, people just accept it as normal and go along with it. It's still in our laws and in our consciousness and I think we need to stop it."

"Have you ever thought some people just want the comfort of knowing that there's somebody on this planet that loves them so much and that they're so sure of that love, they're willing to tell the world and sign a contract to say they will have that love forever? Is that not romance?"

"For some, maybe, but it's rare," I say.

"And was our love not rare enough for us to take that step?" Rosemary says, looking down as she plays with the cup.

"Our love was real. You know that."

"Do I?" Rosemary says, looking up from the cup to look at me.

"Yes," I nod.

"It doesn't feel like it now," Rosemary says, once again looking down at her cup.

"You're missing the point Rosemary; you always miss the point."

"What is the point Johnny? Because all I can hear is the ramblings of a very sad man."

"The point is every day all I see is people together, getting married and they're just all following on the same path because nobody else chooses to be any different and part of me wants everybody to be different so I can do what I want and feel like it's okay and it's normal."

There's a slight silence as I try to think what I want to say, knowing full well I can't explain it well.

"People want to be like their parents, or their family, or their friends. So, when everybody around them does the same thing, it's natural for them to feel like that is something they must do. It's like being alone or single or childless is frowned upon but I think it should be applauded. Applauded because you're not bowing down to society's pressures to be like everybody else. But it's tough to be that person because you want to be invited out. You want to be invited out with your mates, but now your mates are going on couples' holidays, and couples' days out and you're excluded. Now you feel like shit and the only time you don't feel like shit is when you find yourself in a relationship with a person which now means you get invited to places and you're all one big happy family and you can never leave because you'll go back to never being invited again."

"And did you feel like that with me?" Rosemary bluntly asks.

"No, I didn't."

"So, you must feel like that with Ava now then and if that's the case, it's a conversation you should be having with her."

"It's not like that; it's just a thought about the way things are and how life is just a bit shit, no matter what you decide."

Rosemary shakes her head, then speaks.

"I kissed someone the night I went out with your sister. I know I kissed them because I found a piece of paper with somebody's number on it in my handbag a few days later. I had a flashback of dancing on the dancefloor alone whilst your sister went to the toilet and somebody coming up to dance with me and then kissing me."

"What the fuck?" I can't believe what I've just heard.

"Life is a bit shit no matter what you decide, right? So, I've decided to tell you the truth," Rosemary says.

"Who?" I ask, with an anger in my stomach that hurts.

"I don't know," Rosemary says, looking around as I start to raise my voice.

"You don't know?" I shout, standing up as I do so. "So you gave me all that shit over Ava, when you cheated on me first?"

"Don't you fucking dare!" Rosemary shouts under her breath. People are now looking over.

"What? It's the truth," I say, breathing heavily.

"It's not the truth; we're not fucking school kids who can't get over a damn meaningless kiss. It was a drunk kiss, that I barely remember, when I was completely gone from vodka and shots," she says, getting closer to my face as we argue.

"So why didn't you tell me, if it was meaningless?"

"Because it was meaningless, and by the time I remembered, it was not worth the aggro. How dare you! How fucking dare you compare me doing something like that to you cheating on me! You cheated on me with your heart, and my heart was never ever anybody else's apart from yours."

"Just your body was. Just your lips; they were shared around."

"Fuck you Johnny," Rosemary shouts, and slaps me in the face.

Davey D, who has been watching tentatively, runs over and intervenes in between us.

"Guys please," he begs.

"Fuck off Dave; your wife shagged your dad," I say as I try to walk around him to get to Rosemary.

"Don't talk to him like that you prick!" Rosemary screams at me.

Dave turns to Rosemary and tries to calm her down.

"Rosemary, please calm down; let's go and find you somewhere on the other side of the room to sit," Dave appeals.

Rosemary listens, looks at me and then starts walking away with Dave, his arm on her shoulder.

"This isn't over Rosemary," I shout, as the rest of the room looks over at me. I look around at them, then walk back to where I was sitting before Rosemary came over. I lie down with my back against the wall, flicking the cup over that was still sitting on the floor.

Frustrated, I'm shaking. I've got the urge to get up and continue the argument with Rosemary but before I can decide on what to do, I see Dave turn the corner and walk towards me. I'm not in the mood for a lecture from this idiot, so I close my eyes and pretend I'm asleep. As he gets to me, he hovers. I can feel him standing over me; then I feel something touch me, so I slightly open my eyes. He's put a blanket on me. I open my eyes completely to see him walking away to the other side of the room, where he sits next to Rosemary and puts another blanket over her. He sits down beside her and she rests her head on his shoulder as she goes to sleep.

Do you ever ask yourself the question: 'Why am I one of those dickheads who gets themselves into dickhead predicaments?' I'm asking myself that very thing right now. I just act sometimes without thinking. I act without a plan and I end up right where you would expect me to be, in trouble. I've come to the arse-end of nowhere, without a plan and I'm currently sat here alone, whilst everyone else around me sleeps. There's a man snoring to my right and every time he breathes out, more and more snot leaves his nose. In the last hour, it has dribbled down to his third chin.

Bored, irritated and tired, I decide to leave. After hours of sitting here listening to the storm come and go, the sun breaking through a gap in the boarded-up window is my sign to get up and get home. Before I leave, I quickly check the room where Samuel is sleeping. I kiss him on the head and sneak out of one of the side doors. I walk away from the village hall, bag in hand, head down, slightly defeated.

"I've always trusted you," I hear from behind me. It's Rosemary.

"What?" I turn and ask her.

She walks closer to me. I walk closer to her.

"I've always trusted you, from the beginning. It didn't grow; you didn't earn it. I just did and that's why it hurts more," she says.

Rosemary looks at me and I see in her eyes that she also knows that it's time for both of us to say 'no more'. No more shit. No more tears, no more fights, no more banging our heads against the wall; no more going around in circles hoping it will lead us somewhere different than the miserable destination we always arrive at.

"The night I went out with your sister, you rented out a film called *The 400 Blows*; do you remember that?" Rosemary asks.

"Vaguely," I say.

"Well, when I was hungover the next morning, I watched it."

"Why?" I ask.

"Because I thought you were ordering porn films Johnny, so I clicked on it," Rosemary says. I try not to make light of it, so stay silent.

"The main character gets kicked out of school because he plagiarised a writer called Balzac. Remember you used to tell me that if I didn't know who someone was, I should google them because it's better to know a reference than just ignore it or pretend to know?"

"That does sound like something I would say," I smile, with my mouth closed.

"I looked him up and he has written many things, but one thing in particular that he wrote stayed with me. It was relevant to me.

I guess that's what all great writers do: write things that make us feel like they are talking about us."

"What did he write?" I ask.

Rosemary looks at me; she seems calm, composed and at peace.

"Marriage must incessantly contend with a monster that devours everything: familiarity," she says.

There's a slight silence between us.

"And we were married really weren't we?" Rosemary asks, not looking for a reply. "I'm not sure we needed a piece of paper to tell us that. But it was routine and familiarity that killed us in the end," she says, holding herself and rubbing her arms as the cold wind blows into her.

I just nod, and I walk away. I don't know if she has walked back in, or is watching me as I leave, but I know I can't look back and see somebody whose heart I've disappointed. It's fucking painful.

People disappoint people all the time. I've been disappointed and I have been a disappointment. I disappoint people because I'm an addict. I'm addicted to my own misery and if I don't have it then I feel lost because I don't know who I am without that sinking desperate feeling surrounding me. I'm drowning in my misery and refuse to swim because I don't know where I'll end up. The drowning is almost a comfort, because it's familiar. Familiarity is comforting. In relationships or in one's own battle with inner demons, but it doesn't mean the comforting feeling isn't a dangerous one. I recognise the feeling of drowning like I recognise falling asleep next to somebody who I no longer love like I used to. Both instances need me to act in order to live. Some people never do, and they die.

I feel disappointment when I reach out to people for help and the help is not forthcoming. They believe my predicament is my fault and I should be the one who gets myself out of it. I've felt it with my mum sometimes, and I felt like it with my dad when he was alive. That whilst I knew they loved me, they weren't mentors or people who guided me when I needed help. I've resented them for that during parts of my life. 'Well, here I am', I sometimes think to myself. I'm looking directly at someone and they can see that I'm in need of help and instead of helping, they tell me about themselves. They tell me about their problems, or their issues. Or they might try to teach me a lesson. They're not even making excuses for why they can't help but they are outright telling me that they won't because I need to find my own answers. Is me standing in front of a human being, swallowing my pride, showing them that I need help, not me trying to get myself out of trouble? Funny thing is, if someone needed a place to stay, money in their pocket to feed themselves or just an ear to listen, I feel like I've always been someone you can rely on in that sense. Helping is easier said than done of course. Especially when we live in a selfish cynical society. But we also now live in a society where people profess to care about mental health but then turn a blind eye when it involves their participation. People will see a friend in dire need, but the hassle of helping deters them. Then weeks later, those same people will be amongst the first set of mourners writing 'RIP' statuses on social media. God, those people fuck me off. It's as if sympathy likes on a status is the new orgasm. On both sides. The giver and the receiver. People actually also get off from other people writing 'sorry for your loss' to them and I'm now certain there's folk just waiting around urging someone who once said hello to them to die so they can get the thrill of getting a few likes from another vacuous post.

The signal around here is a myth. I've had to walk miles just to be able to order a taxi to come and pick me up and take me to the bus station. Walking around here is peaceful though. There's a calm after the storm today, which is somewhat of a metaphor for my life's current state. The gusts of wind are weaker but still present as I come to a halt at a mini stone path which leads into a field. The views from here are wonderful. I breathe the fresh air deep into my lungs and look around to see the steep green hills and a stream running through the village. It's easy to forget how beautiful the world is sometimes when you wake up to the same walls and sounds every day. I decide to follow the path around and eventually end up at a mini roundabout-like junction. In the middle of the path, I can see flowers resting up above two plaques which are sitting in the shade caused by one big tree and a skinnier tree which have grown in the same area. The plaques are almost resting up against a big stone and I notice the one on the left is written in English and the one on the right is written in Welsh. I get closer and lean over the bars (which surround what I now realise is a grave) so I can read what is written. I read it out loud to myself as I take in the words.

'IN THE 13TH CENTURY, LLYWELYN, PRINCE OF NORTH WALES, HAD A PALACE AT BEDDGELERT. ONE DAY HE WENT HUNTING WITHOUT GELERT "THE FAITHFUL HOUND" WHO WAS UNACCOUNTABLY ABSENT. ON LLYWELYN'S RETURN, THE TRUANT STAINED AND SMEARED WITH BLOOD, JOYFULLY SPRANG TO MEET HIS MASTER. THE PRINCE ALARMED HASTENED TO FIND HIS SON, AND SAW THE INFANT'S COT EMPTY, THE BEDCLOTHES AND FLOOR COVERED WITH BLOOD. THE FRANTIC FATHER PLUNGED THE SWORD INTO THE HOUND'S

SIDE THINKING IT HAD KILLED HIS HEIR. THE DOG'S DYING YELL WAS ANSWERED BY A CHILD'S CRY. LLYWELYN SEARCHED AND DISCOVERED HIS BOY UNHARMED BUT NEAR BY LAY THE BODY OF A MIGHTY WOLF WHICH GELERT HAD SLAIN. THE PRINCE FILLED WITH REMORSE IS SAID NEVER TO HAVE SMILED AGAIN. HE BURIED GELERT HERE. THE SPOT IS CALLED BEDDGELERT.'

As the story sinks in, I hear a car horn beep loudly. I look up, to see my taxi driver in the distance waving at me. Home time.

CHAPTER 10

Remember that show *Home is Where the Heart is*? Rosemary bought a decoration for the kitchen a few years after living together which says 'Home is Where the Fart is'. I smile at it one last time as I put it in the box marked 'charity'. It's moving out day, and the final few pieces of the life I built within these walls are being put in the bin.

I've never been a fan of charity. It bugs me. *Comic Relief, Children in Need*, all those other bloody shows where rich celebrities try to pull on our heartstrings and ask us for money. Piss off. Been going on for years and there doesn't seem to be any difference. Making poor people feel guilty by showing clips of children dying and then a millionaire or billionaire pops up on screen telling you that your last pound could save this kid's life. Of course, people do it because we have a conscience and a heart unlike these celebrities who just do the show to promote their new album or do it so you think they work to protect kids instead of abusing them whilst their other famous friends keep it under wraps. How much did Jimmy Saville raise for charity again?

My other gripe with charity is those people who pretend to care about it and decide to do some shitty charity event in the guise of making money for cancer or AIDS or the blind. Whatever they're pretending to give a shit about, I know they're lying. People care about themselves. Do you think I'm going to buy that somebody is doing a marathon or a bike ride or is climbing a mountain because they want to make money for a charity? They're doing it because they want to do that thing. They want to do it for their own sense of achievement and they're not thinking about the local orphanage when they're posting up all the photos of themselves with a medal around their necks. It's the taps on the back that people want, not the money for charity.

Anyway, a few things are being taken to charity. Ava and I may not be on speaking terms but she text me earlier saying *'Don't forget to take your shit to charity and DO NOT put it in the bin'*. She's angry with me for rushing to Wales to have it out with Rosemary; she's asked me to give her some space, but she still cares about the needy. I don't. I am the needy. Sometimes, however, I've learnt it's just easier to do what a woman says than face the consequences that will come if you don't.

Moving out is a rubbish feeling. You start to remember all the good times you had and how some ugly bastard is going to move in and walk where you used to walk and take a shit in your toilet. You obviously also think about the bad times, and how although you never thought you could, you got through them. The walls still remember the screams, the pain and the tears, but you don't remember them as clearly anymore. I think of this as I reach into my wardrobe to pull out a stack of papers, mainly built up of bank statements and bills. As I go to drop them into a box so I can take them with me, an envelope with 'Gerry' written on the front falls onto my feet. I look down and pick it up. I open the envelope and take out the letter which is inside. I contemplate whether I want to read it, but only because I remember roughly what it says. I wrote it.

Gerry.

This is not a punishment. I'm very very sorry that you are the one that I've chosen to find me. I could try to gather the words to explain why I've put you personally in this position, but to you, I know, the reason won't matter. I also know you won't forgive me for this decision, for how it will affect you and how it will hurt everyone else. I'm still sorry.

You will find me at the park near our place. There's a little bench dedicated to someone called Klara on the path leading up to the football pitches. Behind the bench is a bush which you can squeeze through to get to a small stream which runs through the park. I'll be there by the time you read this.

Please apologise on my behalf to Cheryl. She's been a great help to myself and Rosemary this past year and I don't want anybody to think this is down to a lack of help or support.

Mum and Katie. I love you both. This is not your fault, and this is just something I've been thinking about for a while and have decided to do. I know you're going to be confused and angry with me. Don't be. Please just try and get through this and be happy. I've done this because it's what I want and there's nothing you could have said or done which could have prevented this situation.

Rosemary. I've loved you since the moment I saw you, since the time we first spoke and every single day since then. I love you today and I'll love you tomorrow. Please don't spend your life hurting. I know I'm a hypocrite and I know that any wise advice from me now will look ridiculous. I am weak, but you are strong, and you can have a beautiful, happy life. I have no belief that there's an afterlife, but I've been known to be wrong. So, if there is, I want you to know that I will hold Lucy every day and hug her for you and we will both watch you as you continue your journey in the world. Don't join us too soon; you have so much more to offer here and you will have an army of support which will help you tomorrow and forever. Lean on them. I'm sorry my beautiful girl. I'm sorry that I'll never lie next to you again."

The letter ended there. The thought of never lying next to Rosemary again, made me pause for thought. It made me cry, for the first time since Lucy's death and out of nowhere I found myself crying in my living room alone. I folded the letter up, walked into the bedroom and stuffed it into the middle of a bunch of other papers. Not seen or thought about it until now.

I read an interesting article recently about men and suicide. It was regarding the widely accepted stats that reveal more men kill themselves than women every year all over the world. There is of course a real issue with men not being able to express their feelings and toxic masculinity may be a factor in that inability to open up. However, the stats are somewhat flawed according to this article. It explained that whilst more men commit suicide each year, more women attempt suicide. The writer suggested that the reason being is because women use less violent means to kill themselves. Even in their time of complete brokenness, they still have concern for their loved ones who will inevitably be the people who find the body. Using less violent options to take their own lives means many have been able to get help before it was too late and many for one reason or another weren't successful with their suicide attempt. All I know is, that day, I wanted to die. I never thought about tomorrow because to me it wasn't coming. Maybe, something in me wanted to be alive. I've thought about that. Maybe it was the fact I grew up surrounded by women and the empathy and love they showed to those who they loved was in me subconsciously. Maybe it was the reason why I decided to sit down and write a letter, because I knew I didn't need to write one, but I did. In the moment, I just felt like it was the right thing to do. I also know now that if I didn't sit down to write that letter, I would be dead. I wouldn't have had that selfish feeling of something I'd miss come over me and snap me out of the hopelessness. Selfishness saved me from being called selfish that day.

I sigh and take one last look around the place that has been my home during the most important events in my life. I pick up a pen from one of the boxes next to me and I walk into the living room.

'Johnny, Rosemary and Samuel lived here. Happily.' I write on the wall just above where the television used to be. I walk back to the front door to pick up the last of my stuff and go to leave when it hits me, and I'm filled with a gut-wrenching sadness. I walk back into the living room. *'Lucy'*: I write her name with a little arrow pointing between 'Rosemary' and 'and'. She was my first born. She lived here; and whilst she did, she was happy. I look at our names one more time, and then I leave for good.

As I stand on the pavement with the last of my belongings, I notice there is one unopened letter poking out of the box. I use one arm to hold the box whilst lifting my thigh up to balance it which prevents it from falling to the ground. I open the letter with my now free hand and teeth. It's an invite, from Sabrina, to a Prom Party, in London. Before I can read all the details, a white van pulls up on the side of the road and the driver beeps the horn at me. As I walk closer to the van, I see who it is, and I smile. It's Mo.

"Hello mate," I say to him.

"Hello Johnny, I saw you going in and thought you might need some help with your belongings," Mo says.

"Wow, thanks," I nod.

Mo jumps out and runs around the back of the van to open the back doors. I place my boxes inside, shoving the invite to Sabrina's Prom Party into my pocket and I jump into the passenger seat. Mo jumps into the driver's seat and starts the engine.

"You didn't tell me you were leaving," Mo says, as we drive away.

"It was last minute, you know," I say.

"I've seen people coming and going with your stuff, so I realised you must be on your way somewhere new. Where shall I take you?" Mo says.

"Somewhere new, but also somewhere old," I say.

"What do you mean?" Mo enquires.

"I'm going back to live with my mum," I say, almost quietly, like I know it's a bit embarrassing.

"Oh lovely, I wish I could go back and live with my mother; it's cheaper," Mo says, making me feel slightly better about crawling back to my mum with my tail between my legs.

*****

I've been really thinking about my time in Australia today. Probably because I got an invite from Sabrina in the post with a ticket to an event she just organised at a nightclub in Camden. Apparently after we left Oz, she really took off with the party planning stuff and decided to throw one in England. It's an American-style Prom Night where everyone dresses up. Men in tuxedos and women in dresses. Not very 'woke', but them the rules! (As it says on the bottom of the poster.)

I miss that fresh Australian air. The sound of the sea and the feeling of the sun beaming down on my body. I like the fact that the impression I got from the country was that everybody is valued, regardless of whether they work in a shop on the tills or the head of a billion-dollar business. There is a good vibe going and whilst I understand I only caught a glimpse of the country; what a glimpse! People talk to each other on public transport! If that isn't a vibe you want to be a part of then I don't know what would be.

I remember on one of the days in Australia, Ava caught a bug and was acting like she was going to have to be rushed to hospital. The caring man that I am, I decided to leave her and went on a day trip down the Great Ocean Road. Luckily for me, Sabrina knew one of the blokes who ran a tour, and after wasting an hour of my life convincing her to join me (so I could make sure she wasn't sniffing Russian vodka), she finally agreed and so we headed off.

I remember it fondly because it was probably the first time that she actually spoke to me like I wasn't the worst person on earth. She opened up without suspicion and spoke intimately about her feelings in an eloquent way rather than ranting her thoughts into my face.

As the tour bus was travelling through where we were staying, our first stop was actually in Lorne, at a place called Erskine Falls. We walked a scenic route through a forest to get to a waterfall and I spent more time falling in the water than I did being able to step from stone to stone in order to stay dry. Sabrina found this very amusing as she skipped across, getting other people in the group to take photos of her 'for the Gram'.

As I dragged myself out of the water and back on to dry land, Sabrina came back from the rest of the group and sat down next to me.

"You're old," she said.

"Thanks, but I knew that," I moaned.

"How do you know when you're old?" Sabrina asked, sincerely.

"When you've been going to your hairdresser so long that they've stopped charging you," I responded, picking myself up at the same time and putting out my hand to help drag Sabrina to her feet.

"Come on then, I know you want a photo in front of the waterfall for the bloody internet to see," I quipped.

"Of course, I do, but you're going to have get back down on the floor, because I need the angles to catch me at my most beautiful," Sabrina smirked, whilst handing me her camera.

"It's a camera, not a magic wand," I said, as I made my way uncomfortably back to the floor. Sabrina pretended to kick me.

Our second stop, and what ultimately became our last stop on the tour due to how much time we spent having to wait for everyone to take photos with the waterfall, was a beach, aptly named 'Wreck Beach'.

I noticed on the coach that Sabrina had become distracted by whoever she was messaging on her phone as we travelled. She was less interactive with the rest of the group at Wreck Beach in comparison to how she had been laughing and joking with everyone at the waterfall.

"Something wrong?" I asked, as I took off my flip flops to step on to the beach.

"No," Sabrina shook her head, obviously lying.

I didn't say anything. I did want to know what was wrong, but I didn't want to force her into telling me. I wouldn't say we had grown close by this point, but I had definitely grown fond of her. I walked towards the sea and she followed.

On the beach, there was an anchor which was stuck in the ground. As you can imagine, the people I was with on the tour were taking photos of themselves with it, but because I'm not an idiot who needs to take a photo with everything I come into contact with, I just sat down and looked out to sea. To my surprise, Sabrina joined me.

She sat down, knees up to her chest and her face resting on her knees. She sighed one of those sighs that I had become used to hearing. The one which just screams 'I'm fed up'. I knew she wanted to moan about something but she was trying her best not to.

Then, she spoke. "I don't know why I loved him."

"Who?" I asked Sabrina.

"My ex," she said, frustrated.

"Is that who you're messaging?"

"Yeah," she replied, lifting her head up from her knees and looking at her phone.

"If it's any help, from the little I do know, it seems like he's a bit of a clown," I said.

"He is," Sabrina responded, whilst turning to look at me. "But for some reason I keep going back to the circus."

I smirked at her joke. "So, you don't know why you love him now? Or you've never known?" I asked, not fully understanding her predicament.

"It was one of those relationships where we spent all our time saying that we loved each other, and making everybody else aware of that fact too, yet I'm not sure we ever actually stopped to ask ourselves why we were apparently in love."

I sat and waited for Sabrina to speak some more.

"I don't really know what I'm saying, but I think it's that if we spent five minutes away from drinking and partying and discussed the reasons why we loved each other, I don't know if we could have found any."

"So, if you don't think there are any reasons to love him, why do you still message him?" I asked.

"It's that thing isn't it? I'm not just breaking up with him; I'm breaking up with my life. I'm breaking up with his family who have become my family, and I'm basically saying that I'm never going to see all of these people ever again. That feels horrible in my heart, and so I just find myself still latching on."

I stopped again, I knew she wanted to speak some more, so I waited for her without jumping in.

"I just feel like, I've had more conversations with you and Ava these last few weeks, then I have had with him. I don't know his opinions on anything that matters. If I try to talk to him about equality, or politics, or anything of substance, he doesn't want to know. It's all about drinking and partying, and that's not love to me. Our love for travelling is something we have in common, but do I want to travel the world with someone who I can't speak to along the journey?"

I nodded. Obviously because I did understand where she was coming from and could empathise with some of what she was mulling over. I didn't speak though; I didn't offer any advice. She seemed to be dealing with it by herself, finding the answers slowly, and when she was ready to let go, I knew she would. Sabrina wasn't the idiot I first thought her to be.

When I woke up that morning, I didn't think Sabrina was going to be the person I grew closer to, but it was looking that way, until we returned home to find a sick Ava had stunk the place out with diarrhoea. That particular week, she was trying to be trendy and was on a vegan diet. Let me tell you something for nothing, there is nothing smellier in this world, than vegan poos. But as with all great romances, the greatest height you can reach, is not marriage, but to smell your other half's shit and both of you not give a damn. And I didn't give damn, after my eyes stopped watering.

*****

Reminiscing over, I'm still sitting in the van with Mo on the way to my mum's. He is on the second verse of BOOM BOOM BOOM by The Outhere Brothers. If you don't know this song, you're too young to be listening to me waffling on about the peaks and troughs of life, but google it anyway. This was the song people of my generation used to play at the primary school disco whilst running around doing celebration knee slides to impress the gap-toothed popular girl. It was standard practice in the '90s that the girl would tell her friends which one of the bowl-headed haircut lotharios she fancied and they would spread the rumour about Monday morning's playground wedding. I once had two playground weddings in one day. I got married to Sandra in the playground before school started, but by first

226

break, I had pissed her off so much she came over with an A4 piece of paper with 'Divorce Papers' written on it. She had signed her name, and then forged my signature just to make sure I wasn't going to keep her trapped in a loveless marriage. By lunchtime, I was married again, to a dinner lady, who married me out of pity because she saw tears welling up in my eyes when I saw Colin Christiansen get down on one knee by the bins to ask Sandra to marry him. Joke was on him anyway, because he was soon old news when that slut Sandra moved on to someone else, and decades later, his name has gone out of fashion too, so who really came out on top? One day, he will die, and so will his name. I'll die as well, but there will always be a Johnny about. Seriously though, nobody will look at a newborn baby now and say 'he looks like a Colin to me', would they?

I realise, I said 'reminiscing over' and then went straight back into reminiscing about something else. That happens when you get older, I've noticed. Everything seems to revert back to the past, and there is always a story to tell in any given situation. Everything that happens now seems to remind me of another time.

As Mo gets closer to my mum's house and his rapping comes to an end, he turns to look at me as we come to a halt at a red traffic light.

"I remember," he says, with a surprised look on his face.

"Remember what?" I ask.

"When we first spoke properly, in my shop."

I look towards Mo. "What about it?"

"I had a wise quote in my head, from my religious book, and I couldn't remember it."

"But you remember now, all these years later?" I say, slightly bewildered at how he's brought this up.

"Yes," Mo says, with a gleeful and proud smile on his face.

There's a silence.

"So, what is it then?" I ask urgingly, looking at him again for the answer.

The lights go green and Mo begins to drive. Then, he speaks.

"Translated to English, it means: 'And what is the life of this world except the enjoyment of delusion'."

I look away from Mo to ponder the words he just said. I nod. "Nice, very nice Mo."

CHAPTER 11

Gerry was the kind of person who would grab the bill at restaurants and work out how much each person was paying. There are two types of people who exist when going for meals with friends and family. They are the following:

> 1) Tight people. These people want to work out the exact penny they must pay and will only pay for what they ordered. They will spend a hideous amount of time trying to get their 4p change back and will likely ignore the fact that everyone else has also paid for the service charge, which they have not done.

> 2) People who buy eight Mojitos at £10.99 a pop alongside their meal, which was the most expensive on the menu, and then tell everybody it's a split bill.

Here's where I'm at with it. I don't like service charges. If I want to tip you, I will but don't add it on beforehand. I also know that the waiter/waitress who serves me probably won't get the tip if I pay it as part of the bill, so I'd rather forgo paying the service charge and stick some money directly into the hand of the person who serves me.

If you're with your close pals and you've all got a similar amount of food and drink, then I see no reason to not just make it easy and split the bill equally amongst yourselves. Maybe one of you wants to just make it even easier and pick up the bill completely and next time someone else can get the bill. Whatever you're happy with.

The problem with Gerry was he was all of these people, depending on which situation suited him best. If he got the most expensive meal, he would want to split the bill; if others (mainly me) got a bit extra then he would be totalling it up on the calculator until he knew exactly what he was paying. I remember one time, we went out early on in mine and Rosemary's relationship and I put twenty quid into the pot when the bill came, which he then picked up, pocketed, and proceeded to pay for himself, Rosemary and Cheryl with his debit card. I wouldn't have had an issue with that, but my meal only came to fifteen quid and he didn't give me any change. The prick robbed me in front of my face and there was nothing I could do about it because I was still in that 'trying to make a good impression' zone.

Anybody who has a significant other and detests one or both parents of this significant other will know what a difficult life it is when you go over to their house and have to engage with a prick. It's a war and it's one that you know you're going to lose, but, the small battles, where victory is not so implausible, is what you live for. When Gerry used to say 'hello' first, for example, I marked that down as a victory for me.

I can understand the hatred and annoyance a boy can cause for parents when they're dating your daughter. You've held your little baby in your arms and watched her grow into this wonderful woman. Kept her safe, loved her unconditionally, and then, reluctantly set her free like a beautiful bird leaving the nest. But deep down in your soul, over dinner, you look at this boy as he doesn't eat his vegetables, and you know; that this lad, is putting his little todger in your pride and joy every chance he gets.

I also understand that I was never going to be welcomed in like Jesus riding his donkey into Jerusalem, but the truth is, even if Jesus himself was dating Rosemary, Gerry wouldn't have pissed on him if he was on fire. And Gerry was a religious man.

Christmases were the worst. Over the years, I'd have dinner at my parents' with my lot and then I'd go over to Rosemary's parents' house and we'd have drinks and play games. Every year, without fail, Gerry would get something new as a present that he would use as a tool against me. It didn't matter what it was. One year, he got a dartboard, and we were all playing and it was friendly and jolly but as soon as Rosemary and Cheryl left the room, Gerry got a photo of me out of his pocket and pinned it to the dartboard, then preceded to throw darts at it. "I'm going to have so much fun with this Johnny," he said, with a gleeful look on his face. Another year, he bought a camera, with a timer on it. The whole evening, he was making a big deal about how great it was to have a camera, with a timer. "It's amazing what they can do these days isn't it? Hey, Cheryl, you can literally take a photo, and nobody needs to press the button," he said with his Irish accent ringing around the room with excitement. What happened come photo taking time? "Hey Johnny, take a photo of the family." He passed me the bastard camera and made me take a photo with everyone in it bar me. It happened almost every year after that. One year, even his next-door neighbour Suki Malloy came over and she got in the family photo ahead of me. Rosemary used to say to her dad, "But Dad why don't we just put the timer on, and everyone can jump in the picture?"

He used to say, "But Johnny's such a good photographer darling, he does it so well" or "Oh I don't think the timer's working my love." It was, when I scrolled through to check the photos I took, I saw loads of timed photos of Gerry posing with the family cats.

Suki Malloy, although beating me to getting her face in the family photo, was nearly the catalyst of a breakthrough in mine and Gerry's relationship. She was in her 40s, born in Ireland, near where Gerry was born, and had come over that Christmas from next door because she had just broken up with her husband. He, unfortunately for her, was caught having extramarital relations with a man. According to Rosemary, she had been sobbing all day, and the tears had made her Christmas dinner soggy. Gerry, not in the mood to play the therapist, had progressively got drunker by the time I had arrived. After the photograph shenanigans, we sat down to play some board games, where Suki, who looked like she was another loss away from a nervous breakdown, was trying to explain to me what she had already explained to the others for most of the day.

"Sorry for the state of me," she said, wiping the mascara off her face with a cloth.

"No, it's okay, I don't need to know why you're upset, it's fine," I said, reaching into the board game to get the pieces out.

"My husband was cheating on me with a man," she said, emphasis very much on the word 'man'.

"Oh, right, okay, sorry to hear that," I said, trying to look at Rosemary so she would pipe up and change the subject.

"A man. I was left for a hairy bastard man," Suki said, followed by an awkward silence in the room.

"I shaved me fecking arse for that bastard, and he goes and leaves me for a hairy-arsed man, a hairy bastard, a hairy little wanker," Suki continued, pouring some wine from a bottle on the table into her cup.

Nobody said anything; they all just looked at me like it was my turn to have to listen to the troubles of this stranger I had known for five minutes. Yeah, I used to nod and say hello over the years to her if I saw her outside in her front garden, but, I didn't even know her name was Suki.

"So, how did you find out then?" I asked, reluctantly.

"He used to tell me, he was going to the gym, but he was caught by a friend of mine, kissing the bloke in a bar."

Then, the breakthrough. Gerry spoke in his drunken state. "Yeah, she thought he was pumping iron, but it turned out he was pumping Ian."

I spat my drink out laughing. I got up and had to go into the kitchen because I had gone bright red. Rosemary was part smirking, but part embarrassed at her dad's drunken joke. Cheryl was mortified of course and had to console Suki who had burst into tears again.

The breakthrough didn't last long though. Boxing Day came and Gerry had completely forgot about the joke he made. He had also forgot about his triumphant walk into the kitchen which lead to him giving me a cheeky wink and a friendly tap on the back as I was bent over howling with laughter.

I suppose glimpses of hope are all we live for really. When those glimpses diminish into a realisation that hope is dangerous and the outcome that you long for will never arrive, that's when you understand that some people are just not worth your faith. I had faith that Gerry and I would one day find common ground, but we never did. Even when I turned to Gerry when I was at my lowest, it was because my hope that he cared about me, or had any kind of positive feeling about me, was gone. It was as if I wanted someone who didn't care about me, but knew me, to find my body. As I said in the letter to him, it honestly wasn't a punishment. He was just the only person I felt would be able to deal with it. In hindsight, I know it was a sick way of thinking, but I also know, my mind, at the time, was unwell.

Many people will be thinking that my hatred for Gerry was disproportionate. That, he was just a father, who was looking out for his daughter, and in the end, his suspicions of me were proven correct. I would suggest that would be a bit of a harsh evaluation because mine and Rosemary's relationship was more than just what happened towards the end. I hate people who see the beginning of a relationship and say dumb shit like 'that will never last' and then celebrate joyfully years later when their initial predictions come true. That's not really a victory for anybody when that happens is it? In the past, I've probably been guilty of doing exactly what I now hate; it's easy to doubt others. A couple might spend ten great years together and then break up, but the naysayers will be chomping at the bit to say 'I told you so', before the ink on the divorce papers is even dry. Ten years is a long time to spend with somebody in an intimate relationship. So much can happen in that period and people behave like this is just a fleeting moment in time. As if the failure to last until the day you die makes the whole damn era null, void and meaningless. Spending a part of your life with somebody isn't a waste of time just because it ends. It's a decade of birthdays, cuddles, fights, making up, staying in, going out, chasing dreams and letting go of them. It's looking after each other, caring about something more than just yourself. Making two cups of tea, picking up random shit from shops that you think your partner might like, watching them sleep and thinking how lucky you are to have them. It's a decade of worrying that they'll come home safe. If there is a heaven, I know Gerry will be looking down and saying to Rosemary 'I told you so', which makes me hate him even more. Hopefully, he's in hell.

I remember being at school and learning about a bloke called Bertrand Russell (google him). It was he, who wrote: "Happiness is nonetheless true happiness because it must come to an end, nor do thought and love lose their value because they are not everlasting."

Whilst I didn't listen much at school, I seem to remember those words which I never understood back then sticking with me; and on my journey through life, I've learnt what those words mean. Trying to explain what I think and feel as articulately as somebody who went to Cambridge University might not always work well for me, but I'd rather try to explain something with a bit of a rough edge than not try to explain it at all. In this case though, I think Bertrand says it slightly better than I can.

Deep down, when all is said and done, I know there's a main reason why I have hatred for Gerry in my heart and probably always will. I'm not a religious man, and you know that. I detest organised religion and the numerous delusions that have spread into society and made it completely insane. We now have people walking our streets who believe that the word of their God is more important than the law of the country they're in or more important than just being a decent person. I fucking hate religion but I don't need to keep on explaining why it's stupid and idiotic. I don't need to explain why having a child and then indoctrinating them with your beliefs (which you only believe because you were most likely also brainwashed by the people who brought you up) is wrong on so many levels. Babies cannot be Christian or Muslim or Hindu or whatever other man-made concept is bestowed upon them by adults who should know better. My daughter Lucy was not part of a religion. She was just an innocent baby who died without having the chance to live. Yet because of Gerry, I had to sit in church and listen to scripture about God forgiving her sins and that she had gone to a better place.

Gerry, behind my back, influenced a grieving Rosemary to have Lucy baptised. Some shit about only the baptised being allowed into heaven. What sick fuck plays on their daughter's emotions like that? His granddaughter had just died, and instead of looking after his daughter, his priority was to convince her into allowing his local priest to baptise Lucy at the hospital whilst I was in the waiting room having declined to say goodbye. His stupid feelings came first and fuck what Rosemary and I thought. When I found out, I had so much anger inside of me that I could have killed him there and then, but I didn't. I didn't shout; I didn't scream in his face and tell him what I thought of him. I just looked at Rosemary as if to say 'why did you allow him to do this?' And then I walked away. I went back to the flat and dismantled Lucy's cot and cleared up any trace that she had been in our home. From that point onwards, I felt like I was alone in dealing with my grief.

*****

238

As Mo pulls up outside my mum's, I notice that my sister Katie is waiting for me with a gloating smirk on her big gob. It isn't that she is enjoying my misery, just that she slightly revels in the fact that I'm the one who is having to move back home. When we were younger, I used to make jokes that she would be living with our mum forever, and she would never leave. Sometimes jokes come back to bite you in the arse!

"Johnny," she says, as she takes a few boxes off me, still grinning from ear to ear.

"Katie," I say, as I turn back to reach into the van. I put my remaining boxes down on the ground and look at Mo who is still sitting in the driver's seat.

"I would help you carry the boxes but I have to be somewhere and I'm already late," Mo says.

"No problem, thank you for the lift mate," I say.

"Pleasure is mine," Mo says, turning on the engine and looking behind him to check for oncoming traffic.

"Where you off to then?" I ask, as I close the door of the van and look through the window.

"Nowhere special," Mo says. "Just pottery club."

Mo drives off. Leaving me to stand there watching him disappear into the distance. I walk back to the house, boxes in hand.

"Pottery Club?"

CHAPTER 12

I'm sitting on the sofa watching television with my mum. I often wonder whether I'm the only person who is nearing 40 and has started to have that overwhelming epiphany feeling about life being short. I keep thinking about how the world is going to continue when I no longer exist and I'll never know what happens in it. I keep on thinking about a time when I won't be able to sit on the sofa with my mum and it makes me sad. Or maybe even a time where she is sitting on the sofa without me because I've gone. It's weird to think that the world continues without you isn't it?

I suppose I'm having these thoughts because I'm back living at home. I'm now the age where I actually remember having conversations with my mum and dad when they were this age. I used to think they were super old but now I've come to realise that they had their whole lives in front of them even back then. I often wonder if my mum misses my dad. She's a tough one to read and we've never really discussed him or Lucy passing away. She has a photo of Lucy sitting up on the shelf near the fireplace though, so my mum must think about her when she sees the photo every day.

As my mum has got older, she has started to discuss the idea of an afterlife more and more. She told my sister that she thinks heaven is just a place where everybody is their best self. That kind of worries me. I don't want to watch my mum in her 25-year-old body going to the heaven nightclub where my mates are going to be in their 25-year-old horny bodies. Also, I don't mean Heaven Nightclub in Charing Cross; I mean the nightclub in my mum's version of heaven. On a cloud. To explain this to the youth: a cloud, is one of the white fluffy things in the sky that look like cotton. My mum's perfect heaven is not in storage space on the internet.

I do wonder what my perfect heaven would be like even though I do know in my heart that it doesn't exist. When I was with Rosemary and felt like I was close to death, I thought about it a lot. My main deliberation was in regards to if I died and Rosemary met somebody else, and then eventually died, who would Rosemary be with in heaven? Would she ditch the new guy and be with me? Or would she get to heaven and have to explain that she's now in love with somebody else and I'd have to get on the heaven version of Tinder? Fuck knows.

In my heaven, I'd feel safe. Safe to live. I think when you suffer with depression and anxiety, it's that lack of safety that makes it incredibly difficult to experience life to the fullest. Fear is fucking debilitating. Fear is death without the funeral. My heaven, would let me get to sleep tonight, because I wouldn't have to worry about one of my family members being hurt or being killed. I wouldn't have to worry about cancers growing inside of me that I don't know about. I wouldn't have to worry about getting hit by a bus and whether I was wearing clean underwear or not when they rushed me to the hospital. I wouldn't have to worry about hurting people's feelings. And it's that, which makes me know my perfect heaven doesn't exist. People's feelings get hurt, and that's life.

I do love my mum. She hasn't always been there for me at the right time or in the right way, but, she's still cool. She might mark herself safe on Facebook from terrorist attacks and earthquakes that she is nowhere near, but, that's just her. I am partly me because of the way she is. She's an observationist and nobody observes and dismantles people's behaviour more than I do. I observe other people and observe myself. Even earlier tonight, my mum turned to me and said, "Why do people take photos of strangers on trains who have fallen asleep and post them up on Facebook and Twitter with the caption 'what a weirdo'? They're the fucking weirdos. They're the ones who are taking a photo of some poor cunt who has just snoozed off. You've got dickheads on social media taking photos of people's feet because they don't like the shoes they're wearing, people

243

taking photos of people who look a bit scruffy; yet the actual weirdos who are taking secret creepy photos of people in public cannot see the irony of calling somebody else weird."

Fair point well-made Mum.

As we sit and watch *Emmerdale*, I feel my phone vibrate next to me. It's Ava. I open the message:

"Johnny,

I haven't done this in a while. By 'this', I mean, writing to you and blurting out feelings like I'm about to do.

I miss you. Obviously. These months without you have been some of the loneliest in my life. I've spent longer time alone, but after experiencing being so close to somebody, the void feels bigger.

I know you're probably thinking: 'well you asked for some space', which I did. I thank you for listening to me. I did need space. I wasn't happy, and I was very confused that as soon as we came back from Australia, you ran straight to Rosemary.

I can't compete with time. If it's me versus time then I will lose that battle every day. I know you love her. In a weird, non-lesbian way, so do I. I love her for being part of your life, having an effect on who you are today. I love her because, who you are today, is the person I love today.

I love you Johnny. I hate how it all came about and that people were hurt, but my love is no less strong because it was found in the circumstances that it was. I know if you were writing this, you would find some clever metaphor, like: 'Gold is still Gold even though it's found in the dirt'.

I don't know. I just miss your face. I miss you being an idiot. I miss us laughing about people being dickheads. I miss you having my back and me having yours. I miss the adventures that we haven't had yet.

I gave Sabrina your address. I hope you don't mind. I got an invite through the post to her Prom Party experience thing. Haha! I've been speaking to her and she's doing well. I told her we haven't been speaking and she said 'you two will be back together in no time; you're meant to be together'. I hope she's right.

God! I sound like such a drip. Are you going to go to the Prom Party? I think I will. Just to support Sabrina.

I'm going to start blabbering on if I don't stop typing now; so, this is me. I hope you're okay and I really hope you come to the party.

You're my dance partner.

Ava.

Xxx"

I don't know why, but the message has brought an overwhelming sad feeling into my body. I just feel really down and the fact I've made another person feel down as well makes me feel like shit. I know that I might not be the most likeable person. People who see the world like I do, and have this cynical nature are not easy to like. I don't blame anybody if they don't like me. All I can do is be truthful to how I see things. As I've said, I wish that I could be delusional to the sadness of life. I wish I couldn't see it like many people can't. What I don't want to do is to project my reality onto somebody else. I don't want to speak too much if it makes those listening not enjoy their time on this earth as much as they would have if they didn't hear my words. I understand that Ava spending so much time with me intimately, not in sex but in conversation, could have disrupted any positive focus she had for the future. Maybe she now too ponders daily like I do. I don't like the thought of her alone, pondering whether I still have feelings for her, or miss her or love her. I need to let her know.

"Hi Ava,

I am planning to go to the Prom Party. I think Sabrina would kill me if I didn't show up.

I know things have been shit but you know if you ever want to chat then we can. I went to visit your mum a few weeks ago for a convo, not sure if she told you?"

As soon as I send the message another message comes through on my phone. It's Rosemary.

"Can you look after Samuel on Saturday, because David has got me and him last minute tickets to a Prom Party night?"

I go to type a reply to Rosemary when my phone vibrates with a response from Ava.

"I guess I'll see you there then? And yes, my mum told me."

I let out a sigh, which captures the attention of my mum.

"What is it now?" she mutters, twisting her body on the sofa to face me.

*****

When I went to see Caroline, Ava's mum, it was really windy. I remember it because my hairline has receded to the point where going out in certain weathers is a problem. Raining, it's a problem; my thin hair gets stuck to my head when it's wet. Windy, it's a problem; my hairstyle which has been manipulated into the perfect style to cover bald spots gets blown all over the place to reveal them.

Caroline gave me a hug as I walked through the door. She squeezed me and told me that her back was killing her from trying to do Zumba so she was back using the Zimmer frame.

I sat in the living room, browsing the shelves and cupboards, which had loads of old photos of Ava when she was younger on them. There was a big photo sitting on top of one cupboard which was Caroline when she was probably in her twenties. She was a bit of a sort as you can imagine. As she wandered in on her Zimmer frame, I stepped up to help her, but she waved me off with one hand and held on to her walking frame with the other. "I'll get there, don't worry."

She did get there. She plonked herself down on the seat and wheeled the Zimmer frame out of the way. "Now, what am I going to do with you?" she began.

"Look, Caroline, I didn't mean to hurt Ava."

"Johnny, if I thought you meant to hurt my daughter, that goldfish Finding Nemo would currently be wondering what a grown man was doing lying on his house."

I was slightly taken aback by Caroline's threat and thus didn't correct her on the fact that the fish she was referring to was just called Nemo and he's actually a clownfish. I just solemnly nodded instead.

"I was going to prank you," Caroline said, picking up a flask from the coffee table next to her sofa.

"Prank me?" I asked. Confused.

"Yeah," Caroline replied, opening up the flask and downing some drink.

"Awww," she sighed. "Whiskey. Want some?"

"No thanks."

"Yeah I was going to prank you," Caroline said calmly. She then put the whiskey back down on the table in a similarly calm manner, which actually came across a bit menacing. It was like she was Al Pacino in the *Godfather* or *Scarface* and I was about to get exterminated.

"I was going to tell you a story about why me and Ava were at the funeral," she went on. "I was going to tell you that actually, when I followed Gerry over to England, I did find him and we had a secret affair. I became pregnant. I was going to tell you that Ava was the child I gave birth to. Gerry's child. Which means, Ava and Rosemary, are sisters."

"Maybe I'll have a bit of that whiskey actually," I said, with a befuddled expression on my face. Caroline handed over the whiskey and I took a sip. I winced as it went down. It was scotch.

"That would have been a mean prank," I said, as I leaned forward to hand Caroline her flask back.

"I know," she smiled.

There was a pause between us. One where I actually, for a moment, wasn't sure whether Caroline was joking or not. That was until she got all the baby photos out and showed me who Ava's real dad was. His name was James; he was in the army. Caroline had met him in a bar in the mid-70s and they grew pretty fond of each other. There was still an anti-Irish sentiment back then and her accent which has gradually dwindled over the years was still very strong when she met the second man of her dreams, as she put it. The first being Gerry. James apparently loved her accent and used to do impressions of her which made her laugh. Caroline told me that he was in the Falklands War where he saw his best friend die. When he returned, he was so down on his luck that she used to find him sleeping rough some nights. Apparently, she would pick him up off the floor and take him back to hers to look after him, but in the morning, he was usually gone. Sometimes, the spark in him would return and they would make plans and be in love like any normal couple. Then out of nowhere, his PTSD would switch on and he would be gone for weeks or months. Often, when he was found, he was not able to recognise Caroline and on one awful occasion, he didn't even remember who he was. One day, he never returned at all. Never got to hear that Caroline was pregnant. Never got to meet Ava. They've tried to look for him over the years with no luck, but Caroline expects that he may have taken his own life at some point. She went on to berate the government and their lack of help for brave men and women who have served the country fighting their wars. We raised a toast for them. Then, Caroline told me Ava loved me. She then told me that she didn't need to tell me off, or question me, because she already knew what my answer would be. She said she knew I was just a man, and men take longer to realise things that everybody else can already see. She said she knew I loved Ava and she knew Ava loved me. "Women take chances for love. They go and pick men they care about off the street and bring them home. Sometimes, they walk into hospitals and take them to Australia."

*****

So, the sofa chat with my mum has finished. It went on a long time. I got some stuff off my chest and she listened. Listened to understand and didn't listen to respond or give me advice that I don't need. It was a good chat. The sighing has stopped and I've gone upstairs to lie on my bed. I messaged Rosemary back to let her know that I am also going to the Prom Party and she sent back a smiley emoji and said that she would take Samuel to have a sleepover at her mum's. I'm looking up at the tuxedo which is hanging on my wardrobe. Then, my phone buzzes. It's Rosemary again.

"Hi Johnny,

I'm just up late and wanted to message you to see if you were okay. Samuel has been missing his daddy. Also, Rosemary's Baby was on television tonight and it reminded me of you. It's weird how no matter what happens, certain songs, books, or films will always remind you of someone. I liked the bit where Mia Farrow as Rosemary says, "This isn't a dream! This is really happening!" It had more significance this time around as I remembered that you said that to me when you found out I was pregnant with Samuel. You retain the most unusual pieces of information. I didn't even realise you were quoting the film until last night when I watched it again. Haha!

I feel like after Wales I've had so much going on in my head and have found other words that I wish I said to you before you walked away. It's like when you're in an argument with someone at school or work and you get home afterwards and think of a really good funny comeback.

I just want to say that if I could go back and live our lives together again, I would speak to you. I would have asked you every day if you were okay. I felt like I lost something that belonged to me and now I realise I lost something that belonged

252

to us. It's difficult to see that sometimes, even now. The struggle is always there. Is it for you? I wish we asked questions about her. I wish we wondered about her more, together. I wish we said 'she would have been starting nursery today' out loud. Instead of both of us keeping those dates in our head then facing the milestones alone. I went to her grave many times and I saw that little gifts had been left and somebody had tidied up. I knew it was you. I came home after visiting her some days and I just wanted to talk about her with you and I never. I know now that you felt the same and it is excruciating to see that so clearly when it's too late. The fact we've never stood by her grave together is just so stupid. Why were we so stupid Johnny?

You know sometimes, I wake up and I just don't want to get out of bed because I'm thinking of Lucy. It can be a smell, a feeling, or just a noise that flicks something in my brain which makes me remember that I had a daughter and she is dead. Dead. I still can't believe it happened even all these years later. I try to distract myself from the pain but it never works. Do you?

I carried her in my body. I kept her alive for all that time and she was safe. Then, she came into the world and she was so pretty and tiny and that smile! Do you remember when she smiled at us? I thought she would always be safe as long as we made sure she was. And we did. Didn't we? We did all we could.

I look down at my stomach sometimes when I'm in the bath or lying in bed, and I see the scars. The scars she caused. I can never escape and I can never forget. Not that I want to, but do you know what I mean? Even when I'm laughing and smiling, at peace, for a brief minute, I'll see the marks that she left behind and it all comes flooding back. She was my girl; she was my princess. She was made from love. And she died.

When I see the scars on my body sometimes, they remind me of how much I loved you. How much I do love you. In spite of everything you've done and because of everything you've done. You gave me my daughter and you gave me my son. You made me feel something better than nothing. I've felt love because of you. Now, I know that you're not religious, and I've not been for most of my life, but I need to believe in something that tells me that I will see our daughter again. Even if that is totally delusional. Because I can't live without that hope. And when I finally do leave this world, if it isn't to go and be with Lucy, I'll be at peace, because I'll never know.

No matter if we grow apart, which I hope we don't, we will always have things in common. Our love for our children, and our grief. I don't want you to be a stranger.

So, today and forever. Love always.

Rosemary/Rose (your favourite flower) xx"

I wipe the tears off my phone screen. And I reply.

"I'm going to go and see Lucy tomorrow. Put some flowers down. Shall we go together?"

I wait a moment. Wiping my face dry. Then, Rosemary replies. *"Yes, I'd like that."*

CHAPTER 13

The day of Sabrina's Prom Party has arrived. I woke up to a beautiful morning text from her which said, *"I better see you tonight dickhead."*

Ava gave her my number, which has resulted in me receiving some kind of threatening gif or meme every hour since I woke up. I have assured her; I will be there. The threats continue anyway.

I feel good today. Like something good can happen at any moment. Of course, anxiety and depression never leave; they just hide. So, the lingering thought that something bad might happen is still there, but I don't try and look for it. It's like I play hide and seek with my disorder. I tell it I'm going to count to 20 whilst it goes to hide, but after I finish the count, I get on with my day. Some days, it comes out of hiding and looks for me, but more often than not, it stays hiding. It's a battle. Anybody who has suffered with mental illness knows that. Every day is a hurdle, and every day, I have to try and be Colin Jackson.

One hurdle I did jump over this week is probably the reason I feel a little bit better about the future. Rosemary and I went to visit Lucy at her grave. We spoke some more and it was really invigorating. It was sunny though, and unusually hot. Which meant my head was sweaty and therefore my hair got wet. As you all know, certain weathers can be problematic when you get older and your hair is not being stimulated by the hair restoration shampoos that you've bought on the shopping channel at 3am in the morning. I didn't mind though. I still feel comfortable looking like shit around Rosemary.

I put down a little teddy bear key ring and Rosemary put down a poem that she had written. She printed out two copies, got them laminated and gave me one. It goes like this:

Ah, how this pain is but a bleak reminder

Déjà vu that we thought dead

The ache it lasts and gets no kinder

Another battle for the head

Reach into my soul old foe

Search for the nothingness you left

Back with misery in tow

This time it's you bereft

You're not the first to touch the cold

It freezes time and hope

But in that stillness, we still grow old

We learn to heal and cope

It's life's habitual lust to steal

To take our endmost breath

I would always choose to feel

Even though I must feel death

I didn't know Rosemary was any good at poetry to be honest. She's still surprising me.

Whilst in one sense I have found a level of tranquillity in some aspects of my life, the way my brain works still means in most situations, I still tend to wander off the beaten track. For example, whilst we were at Lucy's grave, I was thinking about how the longer you live, the less people there are at your funeral. I also contemplated whether it would be better to live longer and have nobody at your funeral, or die earlier and have a packed funeral so people would think you were loved and popular. If I died when I was 16, my funeral would have been rammed. At 25, less so. 35, even less. If I live to 100, all my friends and family would likely be dead and I'd be lucky to have more than one person turn up to watch me slide into the fiery inferno of the cremator. Most people would probably say 'but it's better to live longer'. They're not taking into consideration that the longer you live, also means, you have to attend more funerals. You have to watch everyone you've ever loved and cared about, die. Death saves you from that at least.

I'm not thinking these things in a bleak and dreary manner, by the way. More like someone who is trying to comprehend the 'infinite monkey theorem'. I'm just questioning, and both wondering and wandering. We all have those moments when we get a scenario in our head and think about it too much, don't we? Most of the time we'll never really know what the best answer is. Conflicts are not always resolved. Not much is finite in this world. We are all basically just living a Coen Brothers' movie. We live in these mad situations, which are tense and gripping, but they don't always have a resolution. We might think things come to an end, but the feelings and the consequences of everything, continue. Sometimes, we fade to black on situations and people, but whilst we don't partake in any more of their scenes, the show goes on for all of us. Until the final fade to black of course. But even then, the bigger story continues. One that we just don't get a starring role in. This is shit for people who romanticise happy endings, but we can still be happy that we got to see what we got to see. Endings can be subjective anyway.

I'm standing in the living room of my mum's house. I'm trying to get my bow tie straight in the mirror but it's not working. My mum comes over and tries to wiggle it about and gets it sorted. "There we go," she says, with a twinkle in her eye and a nod of the head like she's just cured a leper with her magical touch.

"Thanks," I say, doing up the buttons of my blazer jacket.

My mum grabs me by the arms and tries to turn me to face her, which I resist.

"What are you doing?" I ask.

"Just wanted to look at you."

"Okay, well, take a good look, because —"

"Oh, and your sister called to say good luck," my mum interrupts.

I nod. "Bye Mum," I say, opening the front door and walking out. Just catching her saying "Bye" before the door closes behind me.

One thing that hasn't changed in all the years of me venturing out to have a dance and a party is the need for some Dutch courage early doors. So, on the way to the prom event, I decide to stop off for a quick drink in a bar next to Camden Lock. Walking towards the bar entrance, I quickly realise that everybody is looking at me and thinking the bloke in the tuxedo is having a breakdown. They're not completely wrong to be honest and I'm doing that half grimace-type smile at each person who walks past me and looks me up and down. As I roam in off the street and enter the premises, I'm greeted by a group of hyenas in the form of a hen party. One voluptuous woman is already wailing in my face and her tits are about to hit me in the gob and do more damage to me than the car crash did. "Take it off, take it off," the Hens howl.

Now, the whole bar is looking towards me, standing right by the door, next to the table with all these women, badgering me into getting my kit off. "I'm not a stripper," I say, awkwardly. One of the ladies with an L plate attached to her face gets up off her chair and grabs me by the arms. "Come and join us, come on, come and sit here."

"I need to get a drink," I say, looking towards the bar.

"Oh, we've got loads of drinks: vodka, whiskey, more vodka, champagne," the woman says.

"Yeah, come on; help yourself," says another, waving at me from across the other side of the table.

"Go and sit next to Lauren; she's lovely," the woman still holding my arm says.

Fuck sake. Lauren is riddled with cancer. She's frail and is sitting in the corner next to an older lady who has a ribbon around her saying 'Mother of the Bride'. I get pushed towards their side of the table and sit on a chair next to Lauren. The mother of the bride reaches over her and taps me on the arm then hands me a class of champagne.

"Thanks," I muster, as the Hen party start mingling amongst themselves, leaving me with Lauren and her inevitable *X-Factor* sob story coming my way.

I look to my left to see her playing with her empty glass. Her hair is all but gone; what remains is so thin you can barely see it.

"Do you want me to pour you a drink?" I ask. She looks up at me and hands me her glass. She smiles.

"What's your name then?" Lauren says, as I pour the champagne.

"Johnny," I say, handing back the drink.

"Thanks," she says, taking a big sip of champers.

"So, I've got your name, Lauren. Who's everyone else."

"Well, the one who dived on you when you first walked in is Fat Tina."

"Can you call people Fat Tina these days; it's sizeism isn't it?"

"Well, if you're fat and your name is Tina, you're going to get called Fat Tina, aren't you?"

I have a think about it and then nod in agreement.

"The one who grabbed your arm and has L plates on her face is Zoe; she's the lightweight of the group and my sister's best friend. My sister is the bride."

"Oh okay," I say.

"This is my mum next to me and she's talking to three girls my sister works with whose names I've already forgotten, but they keep giving me an 'aww you're dying of cancer' type look every time they make eye contact with me."

"You've got cancer?" I sarcastically ask.

Lauren rolls her eyes at me and sips on her champagne again.

"What type?" I say, sombrely.

Lauren reaches over and puts her glass on the table. "This would be a shorter convo if I told you what types I didn't have. It's spread all over."

She lies back into her seat.

"Yeah, I did think to myself when I first came in and saw you that you looked like you were riddled with it to be honest." I say, trying to use humour to gloss over the horrible truth of her predicament.

Lauren sniggers, "Hey, leave the cancer jokes to me." She tries to get herself comfortable on the seat and coughs out in slight pain as she does so.

"Oh, is that your territory, yeah? Dark jokes about your own demise?" I ask, finishing my champagne. I reach out the glass towards one of the Hens who is topping up all the empty glasses. They pour me some more. "Thanks," I say, turning back to face Lauren.

"Yeah, that's my territory," Lauren sighs, pausing for a slight moment, looking down at her knees. "You know what they say: good dark humour jokes are like a child with terminal cancer, they never get old."

Wow. I nearly choke on the champagne. I smile, and also shake my head in disgust at the awful joke. Lauren looks up to see me smiling and she smirks. Her mum looks over at her daughter smiling and she smiles too, then looks up at me and we also smile at each other. There's a lot of smiling going on around this table considering the fact one of them is clearly dying.

"How long have you got?" I say, acknowledging the grimness of the question as I get a mini attack of goosebumps on my arm.

"Any day really. Hopefully, my sister comes back from the toilet before it happens."

"I was wondering where she got to."

"She's in the toilet, probably on the phone to her fiancé."

"Do you like him?"

"He's okay; he's not my type. But he makes my sister happy which is what counts."

"What's your type then?" I ask cheekily.

Lauren thinks for a moment. "Someone who makes me not want to die," she says. She pauses again momentarily. "Someone who makes me want to live forever, with them."

She looks at me. I'm hoping inside that she can't see my heart breaking for her.

"Maybe somebody like you. Someone who likes asking me questions," she says, with a playful smirk on her face.

We both sit without speaking. Until Lauren pipes up again. "Someone who can wheel me about at my sister's wedding."

"Well, if you don't find anybody on Tinder, it'll be my pleasure to wheel you about; give me your phone and I'll put my number in it."

Lauren reaches into her handbag and hands me her phone. "It's next Saturday at 2pm and it's at St Phillip Neri Church; do you know it?"

"I know it very well," I say, as I hand Lauren her phone back with my number saved on it.

"They're going shopping on Monday; you can wheel me about then too if you'd like," Lauren says, perked up from a mixture of booze and my amazing company.

"Now you're pushing your luck."

"My sister wants me to buy a do-rag to go with my dress."

"A do-rag? Like a bandana?"

"Yes, she wants me to cover up my bald head; can you believe that?"

I look at Lauren's head, jokingly staring at it for too long with a sarcastic thinking expression on my face.

"Oh, piss off!" she grins.

"So, you're anti-do-rag…"

"Yes, I am. I want to go bald and free."

"Do it then."

"Argh, but I don't want to upset my sister on her big day. She probably doesn't want to look at all her wedding photos in 20 years' time and see herself standing next to an egg with a few feathers on the top."

I grin, take the last sip of my drink and put it down on the table.

"I'm going to have to get going I'm afraid. I've got this prom night thing that I'm going to."

"Oh, that explains the tux and the bow tie."

I nod. "Yup."

"I'm also going to ask somebody to marry me, which is a bit weird."

"Oh, that's not weird; let's see the ring then," Lauren asks.

I take the box out of my pocket.

When my sigh caught my mum's attention the other night, I was honest with her when she asked me what was wrong. I told her a lot of stuff that I've been feeling and eventually that turned into me asking her if I could have the ring that my dad gave to her when they got engaged. She said yes and so here I am, showing it to this random girl dying of cancer. I open the box to show Lauren.

"OH MY GOD - look he's proposing to Lauren!" a voice bellows from across the table.

I look confused. Lauren is rolling her eyes.

"Lauren, you've only just met him; you're moving too fast," Fat Tina drunkenly yelps whilst dribbling wine down her chins.

"I don't even remember his name," Lauren says. "I'm hardly going to be marrying him, am I?"

"My name's Johnny! Have you got dementia too?" I quip to Lauren under my breath, as the Hens once again go back to mingling amongst each other.

"It's a nice ring Johnny," Lauren smiles.

"Thanks," I say, closing the box and putting it back into my jacket pocket. "I feel a bit old to be doing all of this, but I've got to do something."

"You're not old, you idiot."

"I feel it," I reply, with an almost wincing expression coming from me.

Lauren shakes her head at me. "Do you ever get that weird feeling when you look back and you think to yourself 'I'm never going be 15 again, or I'm never going to be 21 again?' You've had your time at that age and you'll never experience it again for as long as you live."

"Yeah, I do actually," I say.

"Well, if you have thought about it, then you know that one day, you'll look back and wish you were the age you are now. Which I get is confusing because whilst you're all done up in your nice suit, you do look like a bit of a state still."

"Well, that's rich coming from you isn't it?" I say in response to Lauren's quip.

She laughs. "You know what I mean though; you'll always want to go back to a time where you felt good or happier."

"I know what you mean."

Lauren reaches over to grab a bottle of champagne and her glass. She can't quite seem to find the strength to lift the bottle without it shaking so I lean in and hold it for her and tip it slightly so the glass fills up with booze. She takes her drink and continues talking.

"When I was 29, I hated the thought of turning 30. I just kept on wishing I was 25 again. Now I am 30, and I'd do anything to see myself turn 40. But I never will."

I tut, then sigh. I feel so bad for her and she looks so fragile and lost yet full of wit and courage. I haven't got any wise words for her and I know anything I say in terms of hope will be meaningless drivel to her. She strikes me as the kind of person who has already done all the thinking someone in her position could possibly do.

"I'll pray for you," I say.

"Thanks, but I'm not religious," Lauren replies, still drinking her champagne.

"Neither am I," I say. "But it's better than not having any hope at all, I suppose."

We look at each other, knowingly. I stand up, "I've got to go, before I miss this thing completely." I lean down and give her a kiss on the cheek. "Nice to meet you."

"Nice to meet you too," she says.

I wave and then turn around to try and bundle my way to the toilet. I've been bursting to go for a while but didn't want to get up. I open the toilet door and quickly skip to the urinal. I can hear some noise and banging coming from the cubical door behind me but I shrug it off. I finish my pee and I go to wash my hands but as I'm washing them, a man and a woman come out of the cubical. It's Lauren's sister. She has a veil on and a bride banner across her. She and the bloke she's clearly just been banging stare at me like they know they've been caught doing something they shouldn't have.

"Hi," the bride says, looking at me.

I dry my hands off with a paper towel and throw it in the bin. "Hi, I suppose this isn't your fiancé then?"

The man steps in front of the bride and gets in my face. He's only about 5ft-something and I tower over him. "You're right; I'm not, but you're not going to say anything do you understand me?" he says, being about as intimidating as a newborn puppy.

I look down at him, and his hostile expression just irritates me. I'm also confused by his odd levels of bravery considering he looks like a child. It's always the tiny people who like fighting isn't it?

"Mate, I'm going to give you a chance, before I stand on your head, to get the fuck out of here and let me talk to the bride," I say, more nicely than you will probably imagine.

"What bruv? Do you want me to hurt you?" he says, in response, pushing out his chest.

I look at the bride to be. She turns to the bloke and pushes him out.

"What are you doing? I'm going to fight him," the bloke says, as he gets manhandled by the bride.

"No, you're not," she says, as she throws him out and closes the door. She turns around to face me. "What?"

"I was just speaking to your sister Lauren outside."

"And?"

"She doesn't want to wear a do-rag."

"But she has to; it's my wedding. I want her to look nice in the photos."

"I know you do, but she doesn't want to wear one."

"Well tough, it's my wedding; she does what I want. I don't even know who you are!" the bride barks at me. She turns around and goes to walk out of the toilet.

"I'm her plus one for the wedding."

She turns around. "What?"

"Yeah, she invited me to your wedding so I can push her about in her wheelchair."

"Well, she can't just invite somebody to my wedding."

"Well, she did, and you're not going to tell the sick girl that she can't have a plus one, are you? And furthermore, just so you know, if I see her, in a do-rag or a bandana, or a hat, or wig, or any other thing that covers her bald head, then I will stand up in Phillip Neri Church and tell everybody what I've just seen in this toilet. I've embarrassed myself in that church once before and I'll happily do it again."

The bride looks nervous all of a sudden. She nods. "Okay."

"Cool. I'll see you at the wedding then. And for fuck sake, if you don't love the bloke you're with, stop wasting his time and yours. You already know yourself that life can be short."

I walk out, leaving her standing alone to contemplate what I've just said. I bustle through the pub and past the Hens. Lauren has fallen asleep on her mum's shoulder. I look at her for a moment and walk out of the door.

After a short walk, I reach the venue for the Prom Party. I can hear the song 'Splish Splash' by Bobby Darin playing inside. People have rented out limousines and flash cars to pull up to the venue in. Luckily for me, I only live down the road so I can stumble home later when I inevitably get too drunk. I look up at the flashing lights coming from the building and I walk up the steps which lead to the entrance. I'm greeted by an overly happy man and woman who both smile and take my ticket from me. "Just through the doors and follow the music," the woman says.

I must be the only person here turning up alone. I stand still for a moment to pull myself together. I'm nervous. I'm slightly tipsy from the champagne I've already drank but shitting it a bit because of what I'm about to do. Everyone is excited as they turn up in groups. I can hear laughter and happiness brush past with every person who gallops up to the doors and overtakes me. I still just stand and take a moment to reflect.

Finally, I walk up to the door, just as a song that I recognise starts to play. I think for a moment, trying to guess the song from the intro. I feel it play inside my memory like I've heard it before when I was doing something important. Then, I remember. It's called 'That Girl Is You' by Dave Matthews Band. I only know it because Ava used to play all their songs out loud in Australia. I open the doors and walk through them. The hall is packed with people dancing. Sabrina has filled the place with old school decorations, photos of '50s and '60s musicians on the wall, copious amounts of balloons and tables full of drinks and food.

It feels like everything I've ever been through has led me to this moment. Every scene of my life was a lesson and the lessons have led me to this room, on this night, to change my life, and to potentially change somebody else's. It's my Arya and the Knight King moment. But as I catch a glimpse of Rosemary, smiling and dancing away, whilst DJ Dave spins her around the dancefloor, and I catch sight of Ava, dancing alone, but happy, I realise something.

It's never been about me. It's never been my choice. And who the fuck do I think I am anyway? I'm just a man, and not a very good one. I'm wrong more than I'm right and I'm pretty sure what I'm about to do is the wrong thing but I'm doing it anyway. I'll call it romantically impulsive and somebody else will call it egotistical smugness. Maybe they're right. Maybe the fact I believe I can just turn up here wearing a dicky bow and start proposing marriage is part of my problem. And everything's been my problem. I'm selfish; I make everything about me and even now when I'm finally trying to do something good, it's because of how I feel. I love this woman, and I've always loved her from the moment I met her. But after everything, why would she want to be with me? She doesn't need me. Never has. She's strong, she's kind, she's smart, she's brave, she's everything somebody needs to be happy by themselves.

I reach into my jacket pocket and take out the box. I look towards the dancefloor and then I open the lid to have one last look at the ring. This is it. I've had clearance and permission from all the right people. Including a nod of approval from a wonderful woman in this room. I close the box and put it back into my jacket. Is this it? Maybe here isn't the right place. Maybe today, just telling her that I love her is enough.

I start to walk through the dancefloor as the song continues to play. I actually quite like this song. Google it.

There she is. That's my girl.

Yeah. Maybe just telling the person you love that you love them, is enough: sometimes.

LA FIN

Printed in Great Britain
by Amazon

57714085R00168